THE
MOON BRIDGE

THE
MOON BRIDGE

MARCIA SAVIN

**SCHOLASTIC
HARDCOVER**

Scholastic Inc.
New York

ACKNOWLEDGMENTS

I wish to thank my agent Andrea Brown for her faith, my editor Nola Thacker for her immeasurable help, and Harry for his.

Library of Congress Cataloging-in-Publication Data

Savin, Marcia.
The moon bridge / Marcia Savin.
p.   cm.
Summary: The friendship between San Francisco girls Mitzi Fujimoto and Ruthie Fox is changed when World War II begins and Mitzi and her family are forced to go into an internment camp.

ISBN 0-590-45873-6

1. World War, 1939–1945—United States—Juvenile fiction. [1. Japanese Americans—Evacuation and relocation, 1942–1945—Fiction. 2. World War, 1939–1945—United States—Fiction.] I. Title.
PZ7.S2654Mo   1992
[Fic]—dc20   92-2601
                                               CIP
                                               AC

12 11 10 9 8 7 6 5 4 3 2 1   2 3 4 5 6 7/9

Printed in the U.S.A.   37

First Scholastic printing, October 1992

In memory of my mother
Pauline Rothman Savin

Contents

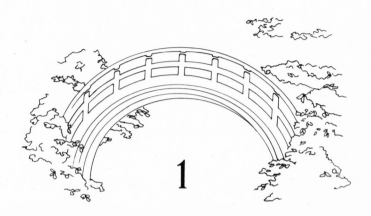

1

Where's Miss Lewis?

"Do you think she'll be here today?" Shirl said, blinking in the wind.

"I *hope* so," Ruthie said, blowing on her hands.

Ruthie Fox and her best friend, Shirley Steadman, were huddled on a bench in the schoolyard of John Sutter School in San Francisco, waiting for the morning bell. It was December and the wind from the Pacific was biting cold.

A week ago Sunday, Ruthie and her family had been listening to the radio when a spe-

1

cial bulletin interrupted their program: The announcer said that Japan had made a surprise attack on the fleet in the Hawaiian Islands, at a place called Pearl Harbor. Ruthie remembered the angry look of shock on her father's face and the fear on her mother's. President Roosevelt had spoken next, saying, "This means war!"

In spite of her parents' expressions, Ruthie couldn't help thinking how exciting it was.

At school Monday, no one could talk about anything else. Ruthie wanted to hear what their teacher, Miss Lewis, would say but she wasn't there. When she didn't come back Tuesday or Wednesday, Ruthie grew worried.

Today was Thursday.

"What if she *quit?*" Ruthie said.

"Ruthie, 'Giraffe' wouldn't quit!" Shirl said. She tossed her head to get hair out of her eyes, keeping her hands deep in her pockets.

"The sixth-grade teacher did," Ruthie said. Ruthie and Shirl were in the Low Fifth. Ruthie covered her ears with her hands. The trouble with braids was they left your ears cold.

"He joined up!" Shirl said. "He's a man, Ruthie!"

Ruthie blew on her hands again.

Thin Miss Lewis was new that year. The two friends loved her. They loved the fact that tall as she was, she had managed to get engaged—they knew from the ring on her left hand. They were sure her fiancé was even taller and handsome and perfect.

They spent hours practicing her Southern accent.

"Is that yuh voice I heah, Ruthie Fox?" Shirl would say.

Ruthie would reply, "Let's keep ouh eyes to the fuh-ront, Missy Steadman."

"Maybe 'Giraffe' is just sick," Ruthie said.

Shirl nodded, but her eyes looked worried.

The bell rang. The girls and the entire yard headed for the large sand-colored stucco building, two stories high with a red-tiled roof. A flagpole in the center divided the boys' and girls' yards.

In the hall on the second floor, Shirl nudged Ruthie.

Miss Lewis! By their door, 208.

"Look what she's wearing!" Ruthie gasped.

"Ssshh!" Shirl whispered. "She'll hear you!"

Miss Lewis always wore a suit. Today she was wearing a dress. It was black.

All of Room 208 quietly took their seats.

"Class," Miss Lewis said at her desk, "I have something to tell you."

Even the boys in the back were still.

3

Miss Lewis folded her thin hands on her desk. The diamond sent out little sparks.

"I moved here to your beautiful city," she said in her soft Southern drawl, "just this year from my home in Virginia. To be near my fiancé who was stationed nearby."

The room was very quiet.

"Sunday," Miss Lewis said, "one week to the day that war was declared, he was killed in the Philippines. Fighting for our country."

Someone started to cry. Without turning around, Ruthie knew it had to be Bev Chibidakis.

"We were going to be married . . ." Miss Lewis went on, looking down, then up with bright eyes, "in June."

Ruthie felt so bad. She wished she knew what to do.

"I just wanted you all to know," Miss Lewis said. Taking a breath, she continued, "This is an awful war. We are all going to work very hard and do all we can to win it, aren't we, class?"

"Yes, Miss Lewis," the class said in unison.

Ruthie wanted to run up and hug her teacher.

"Now," Miss Lewis said in a businesslike voice, "let's all turn to our geographies—Yes, Shirley?"

"I'm very sorry, Miss Lewis," Shirl said, standing up, "about your fiancé."

"Thank you, Shirley. Now, class," Miss Lewis said, "page eighty-two . . ."

As the class shuffled pages, Ruthie wrote a quick note and passed it to Shirl. *Shirl, what you did was so good! I didn't know what to say.*

Shirl read the note and looked up to give Ruthie a small, solemn smile.

At recess, several girls from 208 huddled together.

"Those rotten Japs," said Gerry Trevino, whom everyone called Trevino. She made her hands into fists. "Wait till we get over there!"

"Isn't she brave?" Ruthie said, meaning Miss Lewis. "She didn't cry once."

"I did," said Bev Chibidakis, who was small and round.

"Bev, you cry when you lose your milk money," said Trevino.

"I do not!" Bev said, looking as if she were about to cry.

Thinking about Miss Lewis, Ruthie said, "It was her last chance, too."

Shirl sighed. "She must be at least twenty-four."

"Will she always have to wear black?" said Bev.

"Don't be dumb," said Trevino.

"Well, my grandma does!" Bev said. Her grandmother lived with them and spoke only Greek.

"She's from the old country," said Trevino. "Miss Lewis is from *Virginia*."

"Anyway," Ruthie said, "Miss Lewis can't just throw out all her clothes. She's too poor to buy new ones."

"How do *you* know?" said Trevino, rudely.

"Because," Ruthie said, "she *only* has those *five* suits."

"The gray wool," said Bev.

"The blue serge," said Shirl.

"The green," said Ruthie, "with the gold pin."

"The brown gabardine," said Bev.

"That's only four," said Trevino.

"And the *tan!*" said Ruthie.

"Let's not call her 'Giraffe' anymore," said Bev.

"And let's not make trouble for her," said Shirl.

They nodded sadly.

"Just wait till our boys get over there," said Trevino.

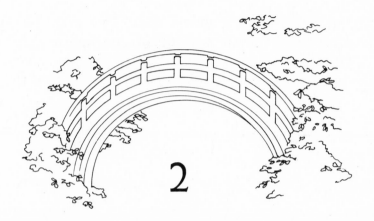

2

Air Raid

$E_{EEEEEEEEEEEE}$! went the siren.

Miss Lewis' class looked up.

It was January fifth of the new year, their first day back after Christmas vacation. Miss Lewis, no longer in black, was wearing her blue serge suit, looking thinner than ever. In her soft Southern drawl she had greeted them, saying, "Class, you are now in the High Fifth. And to show how smart we are, we're having a test."

Everyone groaned and took out pencils.

Then the siren went off. By now everyone knew the difference between the *clang! clang! clang!*

of a fire drill and this steady high whine that meant "air raid."

Ruthie put down her pencil and, ducking her head, grinned across the aisle at Shirl. Shirl pushed hair out of her smoky gray eyes and grinned back. *"How lucky can you get??"* their expressions said. *"In the middle of a math test!"*

The siren wailed.

"Move quickly, class!" Miss Lewis urged as they filed into the hall. The monitors, little Eric Schultz and Bev, carried the special games saved for drills.

All along the hall sat the upper grades with teachers standing guard or checking rooms to be sure all were empty.

While Shirl saved a place by the wall, Ruthie collected their favorite game: a jigsaw puzzle of the USA. There were forty-eight pieces—one for each of the states. The two friends knew the puzzle so well they could finish before the all-clear sounded.

"No talking, class," Miss Lewis said as she visited the other fifth-grade teacher, Miss O'Connor, who was old and seldom smiled. "Uh-oh" O'Connor believed that "rules were rules."

When all the states were in place except the middle ones—Nebraska, Kansas, Missouri, and the Dakotas—Ruthie looked up to see a new girl across the hall. She looked Chinese.

Ruthie suddenly realized that everyone at Sutter was white. She thought all Chinese lived in Chinatown—way downtown.

The girl's black hair was cut short with bangs—like a Dutch boy's—and she was delicate and small. She was playing alone, sitting near the fourth graders, stacking a set of dominoes on their ends in a long curved line.

Ruthie was about to tell Shirl, when two toothpick legs appeared at her nose: Barbara T.

Barbara T. was in Miss O'Connor's class.

"Hi, Shirl," Barbara T. said. "Can you play over at my house today?"

Shirl was looking at North Dakota. "I don't know," she said, pushing hair from her eyes.

Ruthie could see Shirl didn't want to go. She played with Ruthie just about every day after school.

"Barbara T.," Ruthie said, "you're supposed to be with your class across the hall."

"Shirl," Barbara T. said as if Ruthie weren't there. "I've got a new jump rope. Want to play at lunchtime?"

Shirl fitted in North Dakota. "OK," she said.

Ruthie looked at Shirl in surprise but Shirl was pinning back her barrette.

Suddenly across the hall the curved line of dominoes moved. Black tiles were falling, each pushing the next one over, making a beautiful curved snake dance.

"Look!" Ruthie said. Shirl and Barbara T. ignored her.

"OK," Barbara T. was saying, "I'll sit with you at lunch, OK, Shirl?" She looked so happy the freckles seemed ready to jump off her face.

Shirl nodded—without even asking Ruthie, the person she always ate with!

Ruthie picked up Kansas and stared at it.

"That piece goes there," Barbara T. said to Ruthie, pointing above Oklahoma.

"It does not!" Ruthie shouted.

Shirl fitted in South Dakota.

Ruthie knew that Barbara T. wanted to be invited to Shirl's birthday party. It was over a month away but Shirl's parties were always special—never in her home but somewhere in the city. Last year for the circus, only four guests were asked.

Ruthie stuck Kansas in over Arkansas. It didn't fit. She tried it over Oklahoma. It fit.

"I told you," Barbara T. said.

Ruthie was about to say something rude

when Shirl stood up. "When is this drill going to be over, anyway?" she said. "I want my new pencil box and it's in my desk."

"Shirl," Ruthie said, "if you go in there now and a bomb drops, the windows will crash. You'll get glass in your eyes! That's why we have to stay in the halls!"

"Oh, that's not why," Barbara T. said.

"Oh?" Ruthie said, standing up. "OK, smarty, why?"

"It's . . . it's . . . it's . . ." Barbara T. said, widening her eyes, "it's so if the Jap planes come and they look in the windows, they'll think everybody went home!"

Shirl and Ruthie burst out laughing.

Ruthie said, "That's right, Barbara T. We'll just all hide in our basements and put notes on our doors saying we're not home and they'll never bomb us."

Ruthie and Shirl laughed even harder. Suddenly Miss Lewis was tall behind them, saying, "All right, misses Ruthie Fox and Shirley Steadman—you will please see me after school for making a commotion during the drill."

Shirl sent Ruthie her dirtiest look. As if it were all Ruthie's fault!

"You said we weren't going to make trouble for Miss Lewis," Shirl whispered.

"You said it, too," Ruthie whispered back.

With flushed cheeks, Ruthie watched Barbara T. hurrying on her toothpick legs across the hall.

Nothing was happening to her at all!

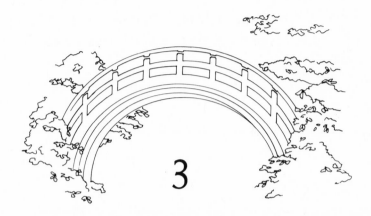

3

The Fight

Ruthie's block was at the top of the Anza Street hill. Two-story white and yellow stucco buildings sat right against each other with no trees or lawns in front. Telephone poles made of tree trunks lined the sidewalk, and overhead a trolley line swayed in the breeze.

It was the next day and Ruthie was headed to school. The morning fog was lifting, letting in the sun.

She passed the large sandlot, partially hidden behind two large billboards that met at the corner, and turned and headed down the hill.

Ruthie was hoping Shirl wasn't still mad and would be waiting at the next corner as always. Shirl had a longer way to come but she was always there before Ruthie.

Three planes roared overhead. Two boys ahead of Ruthie stopped to look.

"They're fighters!" said the first, pointing to the sky. "P-38's!"

"Bombers, stupid!" said the other, dropping his books. "Look at the wings—B-17's!"

Since the war, that's all boys did—argue over planes. Who cared, Ruthie thought, bombers or fighters—so long as they're ours?

Just to be sure she looked up. Yes—stars on all wings.

At the first corner where the hill began to flatten, Ruthie looked around. No Shirl. Just the familiar shops: grocery, drugstore, beauty parlor, and shoe repair.

Ruthie remembered her mother shaking her head last night and smiling when Ruthie described what happened in the hall during Air Raid Drill. "Ruthie," she said, "you always have to put your two cents in!"

Was Shirl late? Ruthie wondered as she waited. Except the one who was usually late was Ruthie. Well, from now on, Ruthie vowed, she was going to keep her two cents *out*.

Suddenly she heard noises up ahead.

Someone was yelling.

Ruthie squinted: Some girls were huddled together.

She ran to catch up.

It was Shirl! And Barbara T.

Who were they yelling at?

Facing Shirl and Barbara T. was the new Chinese girl, staring with frightened eyes.

"Do you eat chop suey?" Barbara T. said loudly.

The girl shook her head.

"See," Shirl said, "she's a Jap!"

"What's wrong, Shirl?" Ruthie said, coming closer.

"She doesn't belong here," said Barbara T.

Stiff with fear, the new girl held her books close to her chest. "I'm an American," she said.

"Look at that!" Barbara T. said, pointing to the top of a doll's head sticking out of the girl's binder. She grabbed it.

"Give it back!" the girl said fiercely, pulling at the doll.

Barbara T. let go. The girl shoved her doll deep into her binder but they had all seen the porcelain lady in a silky green kimono. Its glossy hair held ornaments of thin shimmering sticks. The tiny hand had a paper fan.

"See," Shirl said. "She's a Jap!"

"Stop calling her names, Shirl," said Ruthie, her heart pounding. So the girl wasn't Chinese— so what? It was scary seeing Shirl like this. Why was she being so nasty?

"I'll call her anything I want," Shirl said, coming close.

"It's a free country!" Barbara T. said.

"You can't stay here," Shirl said to the girl. "Go back where you came from."

"I'm an American," the girl repeated. "I was born here."

"See?" said Ruthie, hoping this would end it. "And my father says you shouldn't call people names, Shirl."

"Who are you giving orders to?" Shirl said, bringing her face up so close Ruthie could see sweat on her upper lip. "After you got us in trouble yesterday!"

"You were talking, too!" Ruthie said. Why was Shirl blaming her for everything?

"You're too bossy, Ruthie Fox."

"*I'm* bossy??" Ruthie said. "You're the one pushing everybody around!"

"She is not!" Barbara T. said.

"*Oh, who asked you?*" Ruthie said.

Suddenly from blocks away came the sound of the first bell. They all turned.

16

"Barbara T. can say whatever she wants," Shirl said.

"Well, good for her!" Ruthie said. "You belong together. You both act like brats!"

"Who cares what you think, Big mouth!" Shirl said as she and Barbara T. ran off.

Ruthie's face burned.

After a minute, she looked around. Where was the new girl?

Gone.

Ruthie took off for school, her heart beating fast. Shirl's angry face and words burned in her head. In two years of friendship, she had never seen her like that.

What's the matter with her, anyway?

She makes me sick, Ruthie thought.

Still, as she walked to school, Ruthie was scared. She didn't want to lose her best friend.

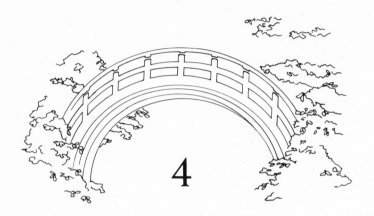

4

Whose Game To Play?

All morning Ruthie couldn't get over the way Shirl had acted. When the recess bell sounded and her classmates spilled out the door, Ruthie walked behind.

In the yard Barbara T., with her new white jump rope, was choosing players for her game. Next to her stood Shirl, pushing hair from her gray eyes.

Alone, by the wall, stood the Japanese girl.

All the trouble she caused! Ruthie told herself.

She thought back to Christmas vacation

when she and Shirl played Monopoly all day with Shirl's new set. Ruthie had gotten one, too, but they couldn't play at her house because her mother had just taken a job selling gloves downtown at the Emporium.

Ruthie had described to Shirl how her father didn't want her mother to work. " 'I earn enough money,' " Ruthie said in a deep voice. "But my mother said, 'With so many men joining up, I want to do my part!' "

The girls had laughed at how Ruthie's mother just went down and signed up over her father's objections.

Ruthie was always amazed at how Shirl's house was filled with furniture—the carpets had little rugs of their own; the curtains were covered with other curtains. The Steadmans' huge Christmas tree had so many ornaments, icicles, and lights you had to look hard to see any needles. Pictures of the family were everywhere. Shirl and her little sister smiled back at you from Des Moines, Houston, and D.C. Their father was an army captain.

Remembering now, Ruthie felt the loss of the long afternoons at Shirl's, playing and talking. Long afternoons with lovely smells of pine needles and something baking, and hours ahead before she had to go back to her empty house.

Barbara T.'s group was chanting: *"Fudge, fudge, tell the judge, Ma-ma's got a newborn ba-by."*

Ruthie looked to see Shirl jumping. The others would have a long wait.

Ruthie silently chanted with them: *"Wrap it up in tis-sue paper, send it down the ele-vator, first floor, second floor—"*

"Hey, Ruthie, feel my muscle!"

It was Trevino flexing her arm to show off her bicep.

Ruthie didn't want to feel it. "It's real big, Trevino," she said.

"Seven, eight—," they chanted.

As Shirl jumped, suddenly her eyes caught Ruthie's and she narrowed them meanly. Ruthie looked away.

It's great to have a best friend, Ruthie thought . . . until things go wrong. Well, Barbara T.'s wasn't the only game. Jump ropes were turning all over the yard.

"TWENTY-ONE—!" Ruthie heard Barbara T.'s group yell in excitement behind her.

She didn't want to turn around but twenty-one jumps was just about the record. She turned.

Shirl saw her and stumbled, and was out.

Uh-oh, Ruthie thought. Now she'll blame me.

But as Shirl replaced a girl at the rope end, her flushed face wore a satisfied smile.

Ruthie wondered if she would still be invited to Shirl's party.

She started over to Bev's game when the bell rang. As Ruthie headed up the stairs she saw the new girl again—on the wrong stairs. She was smiling in embarrassment as a teacher explained.

It's awful to be new, Ruthie thought.

The girl spotted Ruthie and waved.

Ruthie smiled back. Kids didn't wave at Sutter.

At lunch, Ruthie ate alone. If Shirl wants me to apologize, she thought, that's too bad. She's the one who acted awful.

For the rest of that week, Ruthie walked to school alone and ate alone. After school she played in the sandlot on her block or bounced a ball in front of her house.

The following week, when Ruthie was headed toward music class, someone bumped into her. The new girl.

"Hi!" she said. "I'm sorry!"

"That's OK," Ruthie said. "Have you figured out the stairs?"

"This school is so big!" the girl said. "Not like my old one in Sacramento. My name is Mitzi. You're Ruthie, aren't you?"

Ruthie had to be a little friendly. Nodding, she said, "Ruthie Fox. I'm part Swedish, part Irish, part Jewish, and part Italian."

"I'm American."

"Oh, don't listen to that Shirl," Ruthie said. "She's really OK when she's not around that Barbara T."

"She's in my class," Mitzi said.

"Barbara T.? You're in *fifth*? I thought you were only in fourth!"

"Fourth!" Mitzi said, her eyes widening. "I'm ten!"

"But when you were making those dominoes swirl like that," Ruthie said, "at the drill? Weren't you with the fourth graders?"

"No!" Mitzi said. "My class was next to them! I was the last in the row."

"You have one minute!" "Uh-oh" O'Connor said at the door. That meant to be in your seats with your music books open to the page written on the blackboard.

The two girls hurried inside. For music, the two High Fifths were combined.

Mitzi seems nice, Ruthie thought, opening her book. When she raised her eyes she saw Shirl down the row staring at her.

Ruthie smiled. Shirl looked away.

Was she really going to be like this? Ruthie sighed and thought, better stay away from Mitzi.

At lunchtime the next day, Ruthie stood looking for someone to eat with. She hated having to glance around pretending she didn't care.

Mitzi was eating alone.

"Hi," Mitzi said.

"Hi," Ruthie said.

"Ruthie!"

It was Shirl, sitting next to Barbara T. down the bench. She showed Ruthie there was room.

Ruthie's heart took a jump. She told herself, she's probably just bored with that silly Barbara T.

Ruthie looked at Mitzi, then down at Shirl. She thinks she can just push me away and pull me back whenever she chooses.

The sea gulls on the sloping red-tile roof strutted and flapped their wings.

To turn Shirl down now would be saying they could never be friends again. And definitely no party invitation.

Ruthie shrugged at Mitzi and went to sit with Shirl.

Barbara T. acted like Ruthie wasn't there.

Ruthie wished things weren't so complicated. She wanted to ask Mitzi how she made the dominoes dance.

"What did you think of that test?" Shirl asked.

"Awful," Ruthie replied, chewing. "Miss Lewis sure goes crazy over geography."

"I missed at least ten," Shirl said.

Which probably meant three.

"Maybe Miss Lewis likes geography," Barbara T. said, "because her fiancé died in the Philippines."

Ruthie and Shirl looked at each other. Barbara T. said such goofy things.

How could Shirl be friends with her? Ruthie wondered. Not only was she empty-headed but she made Shirl act mean.

The next day, Friday, Shirl passed Ruthie a note in class.

Meet at the Alcazar tomorrow?

For a year at least, Ruthie and Shirl never missed a Saturday matinee. The Alcazar showed a double feature, a cartoon, serial, and newsreel.

Ruthie wanted to go but not as a threesome. *Is Barbara T. coming?* she wrote.

No, Shirl wrote back. *Her mother won't let her off the block.*

OK, Ruthie scribbled, trying to keep her excitement from showing. *Meet in front at 12:30?*

24

OK, Shirl wrote back. *See you then!*

Crossing her arms, Ruthie secretly hugged herself in excitement and relief. When you were best friends with someone for two years, it didn't just end over a little fight.

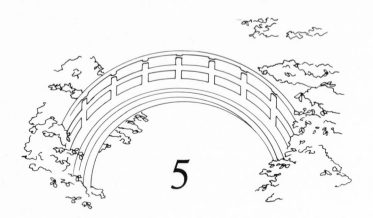

5

The Invitation That Wasn't

Saturday movies at the Alcazar, Ruthie was thinking as she walked to school with Shirl on Monday, had been wonderful. The only bad part was the newsreels showing English children huddled in underground shelters while bombs shrieked and fell and houses burst into flames.

When the two friends came outside at recess, they joined Bev's jump rope game. Trevino was jumping. Barbara T. held one rope end.

Shirl got in line behind Bev, and Ruthie stood behind Shirl.

"Tomorrow I'm giving out the invitations," Shirl whispered. Her party was three weeks away.

"Where's it going to be?" Ruthie whispered back.

"Can't tell—secret," Shirl said.

"Well, who's coming?" Ruthie asked, annoyed at Shirl's air of mystery.

Shirl indicated with her eyes: Barbara T. and Bev. Not Trevino.

Ruthie knew she was included. From the way the other girls' eyes met Shirl's with pleased looks, they knew, too.

Ruthie felt sorry for Trevino. But she couldn't imagine her at a party where you had to wear a dress. Trevino only wore skirts and sweaters.

As Ruthie waited, she saw Mitzi nearby, watching.

Bev noticed her, too. "Come on in," she called.

Mitzi ran up behind Ruthie.

"Hi," she said.

"Hi," Ruthie answered.

"She can't play!"

Ruthie turned around.

It was Shirl. Staring at Mitzi.

Not again.

Mitzi's face went still. The rope stopped turning.

"Yeah, we don't want no Japs around here," Barbara T. said, dropping the rope and coming over.

Ruthie's stomach tightened. But this time, she told herself, it wasn't one against two. Bev and Trevino were here.

"She can't play," Shirl repeated.

"What's wrong?" Trevino said, coming over.

Ruthie looked hard at Bev. Her eyes said, "It's *your* game, Bev."

Bev looked uncertainly at Ruthie then at Shirl.

Come on, Bev, Ruthie silently pleaded, tell them you can let anyone you want play.

Bev shrugged and looked at the ground. "It doesn't matter to me," she said.

"No Japs!" Shirl said, staring at Mitzi.

"Stop calling me that!" Mitzi said, her eyes flashing. "I'm as American as you are!"

"Shirl, she's Chinese," Trevino said. "They're on our side."

"No, she isn't," said Barbara T. "She has a Jap doll—don't you?" she said, turning on Mitzi.

Four sets of eyes stared.

Four against one. Ruthie couldn't stand it.

"So what if she has a doll?" Ruthie said. "Let her play!"

Shirl stepped close to Ruthie. Her face was red. "You're not coming to my party," she said.

"And it's going to be in the Chinese Tea Garden, too!" said Barbara T., her eyes popping.

"Well, I been there a hundred times," Ruthie said, thinking someday somebody was going to pop those eyes right back into Barbara T.'s skull.

"I'll bet!" Barbara T. said.

"Anyway," Ruthie said to Barbara T., "you don't even know its name: It's the *Japanese* Tea Garden, smarty!"

"Not anymore," Shirl said. "It's the *Chinese* Tea Garden now!"

"Who says?" Ruthie said.

"Go and look!" Shirl said.

Tears came to Ruthie's eyes. She blinked them back as she looked at the others. Now it was four against her. Neither Bev nor Trevino opened her mouth. Everyone wanted to be on the side of Shirl, the party girl.

And Barbara T. knew where the party was! That hurt almost as much as losing the invitation.

"Ruthie . . ." It was Mitzi's voice.

Ruthie turned away. She didn't need anyone feeling sorry for her now.

29

"This is dumb," Trevino said. "Come on, let's play."

But Shirl and Barbara T. were walking away and Bev was winding her rope, her eyes on the ground.

Ruthie turned and walked back to class, her face still burning from having the invitation taken from her like that in front of everybody, hating everyone and everything—most of all Mitzi, the troublemaker.

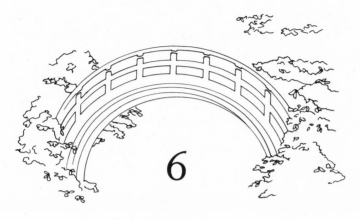

6

Mitzi

That week was horrible for Ruthie. How could Shirl do that to her? Take away her invitation in front of everybody?

Ruthie hated Shirl now and the others who stood there watching her be humiliated.

Most of all that Mitzi.

Sometimes Ruthie tried to understand Shirl's behavior. OK, she would tell herself, Shirl's father was in the army and would have to fight. And OK, Barbara T. was a terrible influence.

But nothing nothing nothing excused what she did to me, Ruthie told herself.

Not only was the friendship through but Ruthie wondered how she could ever have liked someone like Shirl in the first place.

Ruthie ate alone again, kicking her heels under the bench to show she didn't care and staring into space. Not one of her supposed friends had opened her mouth to stick up for her.

Let them go to their stupid party. Trevino probably now had Ruthie's invitation.

When Ruthie went to her new spot on the bench she often passed Mitzi eating alone and pretended not to see her.

When Mitzi said "Hi," Ruthie pretended not to hear.

Sometimes she felt bad doing it, but then she'd tell herself, "Serves her right! I stick up for her and what do I get? A kick in the face."

The following Monday, Miss Lewis announced that the first U.S. troops had landed overseas—in Northern Ireland. Everyone cheered. Shirl stood up and said we were sinking one ship a day in the Philippines.

The class watched Miss Lewis' pointer at the map marking the victory battles. To celebrate, she let them have free reading instead of the test she'd planned.

The first good news since the war started made everyone silly and bubbly. Ruthie wished she had someone to share it with. She sat at her desk trying to be happy. She told herself that someday she wouldn't have to check planes to see if they had stars.

A few days later in the auditorium, under the mural of John Sutter panning for gold, Ruthie listened with her class while the principal talked about how they should all buy war stamps and save scrap metal.

Ruthie was wondering how long before the singing would start. Her favorite was "Coming in on a Wing and a Prayer."

Someone tapped her on the shoulder.

Bev. Ruthie hadn't talked to her since the fight over a week before.

"Ruthie, I feel really bad about what happened," Bev whispered.

Ruthie shrugged. "I thought you were all busy making party plans," she said. Shirl's party was a week from Saturday.

Bev shook her head. "I was on your side."

"Then why didn't you say something, Bev?"

Bev looked down. "I wanted to, Ruthie, but I can never speak up."

Ruthie knew it was true. She knew watching Bev winding her rope after the fight that Bev felt awful.

"Well, thanks," Ruthie said. She liked Bev, but it would have made such a difference if she had said just one word.

"It wasn't fair," Bev said, looking up. "To Mitzi. And losing your invitation."

Ruthie shrugged. "Did Trevino get it?" she asked.

Bev nodded.

"Think she'll wear a dress?"

Bev puffed out her fat cheeks, holding in a giggle, but it broke out.

They laughed together, trying to imagine the muscular Trevino in ribbons and bows. Miss Lewis looked at them and put her finger to her lips.

"I don't care about that party," Ruthie whispered as the words to "Anchors Aweigh" flashed on a screen. She wished she meant it. Not because of Shirl, but to be at the Tea Garden, with its winding walks and streams. To drink tea and have cookies at the open-air tables by the water and rocks where everywhere you looked was beautiful. Best of all wasn't even the looking. It was climbing the Moon Bridge and dropping a penny to wish in the pond below.

That night Ruthie and her mother were eating dinner. Her father was working overtime at the shipyards. They were talking—for the tenth time—about the fight.

"How could I have ever liked her?" Ruthie said, shaking catsup on her hot dogs and beans.

Her mother sighed. She had changed from her black work dress to a robe and slippers, and her hair was loose.

"Honey . . ." her mother said, putting two teaspoons of sugar into her coffee, "sometimes you think you know someone, but you really don't. It hurts now, but just remember—there's always more fish in the sea."

She reached for another spoonful and stopped. Sugar rationing was coming soon and she was trying to cut down.

Ruthie didn't believe it—about more fish in the sea. There was only one Shirl. Now she was gone and there was no one.

Friday, Ruthie was walking down the long Anza Hill through empty streets to school. She was late—she had to fix her own lunch and couldn't decide between deviled egg or tuna. Finally she took deviled egg and now she wanted tuna.

She was probably going to get marked tardy and she didn't care.

As Ruthie neared the corner, she saw that

the mounted policeman at the crosswalk was gone.

In his place stood a woman in a dark suit and policeman's cap.

"Hurry up, Ruthie, you'll be late!" she called.

It was Mrs. Chibidakis! Bev's mother looked just like Bev—short and round with kind eyes.

"You're a policeman?" Ruthie said, crossing the street.

"A volunteer traffic cop," Mrs. Chibidakis corrected. "We've got to help out now that the men are joining up. Better hurry now."

Everything was changing, Ruthie thought. Hating the idea of school, she walked slowly past the cyclone fence. She dreaded sitting in the same room with Shirl.

Up ahead someone was standing at the gate, not going in.

Ruthie came closer.

It was Mitzi.

Her again.

Why was she just standing there?

Ruthie didn't want to talk to her but she had to get past.

Looking into the schoolyard, Ruthie wondered what was wrong. It looked the same. A sand-colored building with sea gulls on the tiled roof and a yard full of noisy children.

But at the edge of the crowd stood Shirl and Barbara T., staring back at Mitzi.

Ruthie saw how frightened Mitzi was—afraid to walk into her own school. Thinking guiltily of all the times she had snubbed her, Ruthie felt awful. All her anger left and she wanted to say something. But then the bell rang.

Everybody from the smallest kindergartner to the biggest sixth grader stood at attention while the four flag bearers, red straps across their chest, marched with the colors to the flagpole. As they unfolded the flag, everyone—Mitzi and Ruthie included—put their hands on their hearts for the Pledge.

". . . with liberty and justiceforall."

The flag bearers marched back across the yard and teachers took their places near the stairs for classes to line up. Shirl and Barbara T. separated and went in line.

Still Mitzi didn't move.

"Aren't you coming in?" Ruthie said, stepping into the yard.

Mitzi stared ahead.

"Come on, you'll be late," Ruthie said. "And

you've got 'Uh-oh' O'Connor!" Ruthie rolled her eyes. "She kills you!"

Mitzi stepped down into the yard and walked with Ruthie.

"Why do you call her that?" she asked.

" 'Uh-oh'? 'Cause if you're not where you're supposed to be and she catches you . . . *Uh-oh!*" Ruthie rolled her eyes. "She caught me in the hall once."

Mitzi smiled. "She seems OK to me," she said. "It's those girls I don't like—"

"Hey, don't be afraid of Shirl. She's got the biggest mouth in the fifth grade. We used to be friends—but she's just too mean. She and that awful Barbara T. They deserve each other."

"*She's* in my class," Mitzi said.

"I know," Ruthie said. "But you don't have to worry about her. Barbara T. won't open her mouth without Shirl."

As soon as the words were out, Ruthie knew she had kidded herself thinking it was Barbara T. being a bad influence on Shirl. If anything, it was the other way around.

Barbara T.—always someone's echo. Whether that person was smart or dumb didn't matter.

But not Shirl. Hadn't she and Ruthie argued time and again about how to do something or what to do? Ruthie had liked having a friend with a mind of her own. But Shirl was nobody's echo. Which meant that what Ruthie's mother said was true: Sometimes we really don't know people we think we know.

"Did she change her mind?" Mitzi said.

"Who?" said Ruthie, lost in thought.

"That girl." Mitzi couldn't say her name. "About inviting you."

"No, but that's not what I'm thinking about," Ruthie said.

"Well, anyway," Mitzi said quietly, "maybe she will."

Ruthie looked at the smaller girl. After all she had been through—she's thinking about me! Then Ruthie saw that Mitzi was afraid Ruthie would blame her for the loss of the invitation.

Which I did do, Ruthie thought guiltily.

"Oh," Ruthie said, "who wants to go anywhere with kids who act like that?"

A small bounce came into Mitzi's walk.

"I been there once," Mitzi said. "To the— Tea Garden."

"Me, too," said Ruthie. "Twice."

"I love the giant goldfish. They're so fat!"

"And drinking tea outdoors from the little cups," said Ruthie.

"And the great Buddha. He's bigger than . . . ten people!"

"And dragonflies! And cattails!"

"And the big turtles!"

"What about the Moon Bridge?" Ruthie said.

"It's so round," Mitzi said. "Like the moon."

"And high. If you don't hold on, you'll fall off."

"It's my favorite place," Mitzi said.

"Me, too!" said Ruthie. The Tea Garden was the most beautiful place in the world and the Moon Bridge was the best part.

"Hurry, girls," called Miss Lewis in her tan suit, from down the hall.

"'Bye, Mitzi," Ruthie called.

"'Bye, Ruthie," Mitzi called back, disappearing inside "Uh-oh" O'Connor's door.

"See you at lunch," Ruthie called, but the door had already closed.

She's a good kid, Ruthie thought as she took her seat in her classroom, for the first time in weeks forgetting all about Shirl across the aisle.

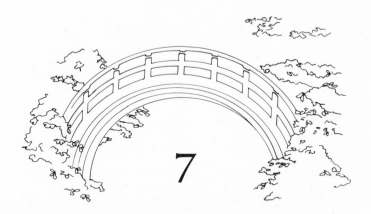

7

Tuna and Deviled Egg

When Ruthie came out for lunch she found Mitzi and sat beside her.

"What do you have?" Ruthie said, pulling out her sandwich.

Mitzi gave a one-shoulder shrug and opened her lunch bag. "Tuna," she said.

"Oh!" Ruthie laughed. "That's what I wanted but I have deviled egg."

"Want to trade?" Mitzi said. "I like deviled egg better."

"OK." As they exchanged sandwiches,

Ruthie said, "How come you just came here from Sacramento?"

"I didn't," Mitzi said. "We moved last summer. First I went to school in Japantown."

Ruthie had never been to Japantown. She had seen it when the trolley went through on its way downtown. Like Chinatown, the streets were crowded with people, some in kimonos and sandals. The shops had signs in both strange writing and English. Like Chinatown, too, Japantown started abruptly at one street, went on for several more blocks of crowded shops with colorful wares, then abruptly stopped.

"Why'd you come here then?"

Mitzi looked down at the sandwich. "This is good. My mother doesn't put pimentos in."

"That's what makes it deviled," Ruthie explained, and repeated her question. "Why'd you change from your other school to Sutter?"

"See," Mitzi said, "in Sacramento where I went to school there weren't any other Japanese. My friends were all kinds. And my dad likes that. He thinks it's good to get to know everybody— not just stick with your own kind."

Well, Sutter certainly had all kinds, Ruthie was thinking. Trevino's family was from Italy, Bev's from Greece, her own a mixture. Many kids' parents or grandparents were immigrants. The one who was different was Shirl, who came from Iowa.

Ruthie took another bite of Mitzi's tuna on whole wheat. She really liked it. Her mother never bought whole wheat.

"You mean you can just change schools if you want?" Ruthie said.

"Uh-huh."

Ruthie thought Mitzi looked too casual. It didn't sound right.

"Don't tell those girls," Mitzi said, "about where I live or anything."

"I never talk to them," Ruthie said. She didn't know if Mitzi meant Shirl and Barbara T. or all of them but it didn't matter. Ruthie could keep a secret.

She leaned back, smiling at the blue sky. "Boy, it's hot," she said, closing her eyes.

Mitzi laughed. "Hot? This is *warm*."

"Warm?" Ruthie said. "I'm getting a sunburn!" She stretched out her legs.

Mitzi laughed again. "There's a girl over there with a coat on."

"Can I help it if she's dumb?" Ruthie said.

They both laughed.

"In Sacramento, we call this winter," Mitzi said. "In summer we sleep in our underwear with just the sheets."

Ruthie couldn't imagine it. San Francisco was always cold at night. From her bedroom window she could see the ocean where the cold wind blew all year round.

"Well," said Ruthie, "here it gets so foggy if you're not careful, you can walk right into a wall!"

Mitzi laughed.

Ruthie liked Mitzi. She was small but she wasn't afraid of "Uh-oh" O'Connor and she knew what was a joke and what wasn't.

Over the weekend Ruthie looked forward to seeing her again.

When Monday came, they ate together.

"Can you play on my block after school?" Ruthie said.

"Maybe tomorrow if I ask," Mitzi said. "But I have to go home first and change."

"So do I," Ruthie said. She often forgot and got lectured.

"Your mother would have to call my mother to say it's OK," Mitzi said.

"She will. She works so we have to play outside. Can you meet me in the corner lot? You know at the top of the Anza hill? With the billboards?"

"Sure," Mitzi said. "Can you remember my number?"

44

"Sure."

Ruthie closed her eyes and concentrated while Mitzi recited it.

"Ask for Mrs. Fujimoto. Can you remember that?"

"Sure. Mrs. Fugi—" Ruthie stumbled over the name.

"—moto," Mitzi said. "Oh, just ask for 'Mitzi's mother.'"

The bell rang. They jumped off the bench, tossing their lunch bags into the garbage as the sea gulls swooped down for scraps.

At one end of the yard Shirl and Barbara T. were unfolding Barbara T.'s jump rope. At another Bev was unwinding hers with Trevino.

Ruthie wondered how she could have thought Shirl looked so wonderful with that hair always in her eyes.

"Hey," Bev called to Mitzi and Ruthie. "Come on—take the ends."

"OK!" Ruthie said.

"You can," Mitzi said. "I'm sorta tired." She sat down again.

She's afraid of another scene, Ruthie thought.

"I'm tired, too," Ruthie replied, sitting down next to Mitzi.

"What are you waiting for?" Trevino called. "The bell to ring?"

45

Ruthie looked at Mitzi. They both jumped up and took rope ends. Other girls from Mitzi's class joined them.

"I'm a little Dutch girl dressed in blue," Ruthie began.

"Here are the things I like to do . . ." Mitzi joined in.

They all chanted:

Salute to my soldier,
Curtsy to my queen,
Jump right over
A submarine!

The game went on peacefully until the bell rang.

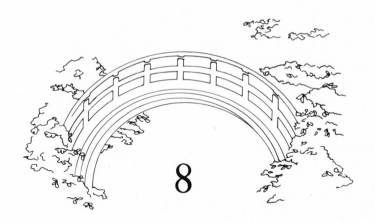

8

The Sandlot

At dinner that night while her parents discussed shortages, Ruthie waited impatiently for her mother to call Mitzi's.

"They're saying 'no new cars for the duration,'" her mother said. "We'd better be good to that old jalopy!"

"How about that, Cookie?" Ruthie's father said, winking at her. "We finally get Mommy working so we can *afford* a new car and now they say we can't buy one!"

Ruthie's mother sent her a secret smile. Wasn't this the man, it said, who didn't want me to work?

Ruthie smiled back and said, "Don't forget to call Mitzi's."

"Ruthie, I haven't finished eating!" her mother said.

Ruthie nearly died when her mother had a second cup of coffee. But finally she called, and Mitzi's mother said yes!

The next day at recess Ruthie and Mitzi excitedly made plans. Shirl and Barbara T. passed them, looking the other way. At least they're not calling names, Ruthie thought.

After school Ruthie stood at the top of the Anza hill in front of the sandlot where the billboards met at the corner. In one direction houses dipped down to the ocean. In another, they sailed into the horizon toward Japantown and the rest of the city.

It seemed forever since Ruthie had let herself into her empty place—she lived upstairs in a two-family house—and changed into her old blouse and dungarees. She didn't stop to eat for fear of missing Mitzi even though Mitzi had to go home and back. Now Ruthie's stomach was growling.

What if Mitzi's mother changed her mind? She sounded awfully strict.

Over Ruthie's head, a soldier on the billboard was waving good-bye to a white-haired couple standing under the words, WILL YOU HELP BRING HIM BACK ALIVE? BUY WAR BONDS!

Ruthie decided to wait behind the bill-boards. It was her special place. Only her legs were visible to the street through the crosshatch slats under the big signs.

On her stomach in the sand she lay watching passing feet through the green slats.

A baby buggy. Running feet of schoolboys.

Across the street the sign at the gas station said: IS THIS TRIP NECESSARY?

Ruthie wondered if she should phone.

Wait—

Ruthie stuck her head way down. . . . It was!

In faded pants and shirt, running and carrying a paper bag: Mitzi.

Ruthie jumped up and ran around to the street. "Hi!" she yelled.

Mitzi was out of breath. "Hi!" she said.

"Come on," Ruthie said, grabbing Mitzi's hand. "I want to show you something."

She took her behind the billboards. "It's my secret place," Ruthie said.

Catching her breath, Mitzi looked around at the shaded hollow where they were hidden and the big sandy lot beyond, full of hills and valleys that promised adventure. She smiled happily.

They took off their shoes and socks.

"Look!" Mitzi said, opening the bag.

Ruthie stared inside.

"Oh, Mitzi!" she said. "Where did you get it?"

"My uncle Joe. We live over his store," Mitzi explained, pulling out two Hershey bars and handing one to Ruthie. "He can get them sometimes. But he only gives them to me special."

Slowly they unwrapped the brown paper.

They took off the wax paper underneath and each broke off a single square of chocolate.

Ruthie closed her eyes. The wonderful dark taste slid over her tongue. "Since the war," she said, the words slurring as she sucked to make it last. "Haven't had any."

Mitzi nodded.

"What's special now?" Ruthie asked, savoring the flavor before breaking off another square.

"I told them about the fights," Mitzi said. "How you stuck up for me."

Smiling, Ruthie took another square. "You know what I thought you had in the bag?" she said. "That lady doll. With the tiny fan."

Mitzi lifted one shoulder in a shrug. "I got tired of her."

Ruthie nodded and sucked chocolate.

"No one was supposed to see her," Mitzi muttered.

"You brought her for company?"

Mitzi nodded. "My mother would kill me if she knew I even took her out."

Ruthie didn't know if that was because the doll was precious or Japanese but she understood how Mitzi felt. When you're new you want to hold something familiar.

"We're too big for dolls, anyway," Ruthie said. "Look!" She unfolded a magazine picture from her pocket.

The whitest teeth in the world smiled at them. Ruthie was always the first in line when his pictures came to the Alcazar.

"I call him 'Mr. Dark Eyes,' " Ruthie said.

"Why?"

" 'Cause then no one knows who I'm in love with," Ruthie said. "Isn't he the handsomest?"

"He's OK."

"Just 'OK'??" Ruthie was hurt.

Mitzi shrugged and broke off another square of chocolate.

"Who's better?" Ruthie asked.

Mitzi smiled. "I can't tell."

"Why?"

"It's a secret."

That wasn't fair, Ruthie thought. She looked around. "What do you want to do?"

Mitzi walked over to a giant cardboard carton lying on its side that said *Zellerbach Tissues*.

"Let's have a ship!" she said.

They turned the carton over, shaking out the debris. Finishing their last chocolate squares, they found sticks for oars and climbed in. The sand around them fell in dips and mounds like ocean waves.

"We're Starving Romanians!" said Ruthie, rowing hard.

"We're escaping the bombs!" said Mitzi, covering her head.

"We just made it!" Ruthie said.

"Watch out," Mitzi cried. "Here comes a storm!"

The Starving Romanians grabbed the sides of the carton and rocked it so hard they toppled over.

"Swim!" Mitzi said.

"Do you see land?" Ruthie said, turning her head from side to side as she'd seen swimmers do.

"Over there!" Mitzi cried, pointing to the back of the billboards as she crawled around the spike-shaped purple iceplant that grew over the sand like a vine.

52

"I see a cave!" Ruthie cried, pointing to the shadowy triangle inside the billboards.

They pulled themselves over, panting, and leaned against the backs of the billboards.

"Thirsty . . ." Mitzi said, gasping.

"All desert . . ." Ruthie said. Then she had an idea. She crawled to a patch of iceplant and motioned for Mitzi to follow.

Ruthie stuck her fingernail into one of the smooth cactus-like sections. A drop of clear liquid ran out.

"It's water," Ruthie said. "I learned this in Scouts. You'll never die of thirst."

Mitzi didn't have a fingernail—they were all bitten off—so she let Ruthie do the piercing. They put a finger to the cuts and licked the precious drops of water.

"Umm," they said happily.

"Let's set up our cave," Ruthie said. The billboards' crossbars made perfect shelves.

Suddenly a sharp wind came up.

"I should have brought a sweater," Mitzi said, holding her bare arms.

"We could go to my house," Ruthie said. "No—wait!"

While Mitzi watched shivering, Ruthie walked around the sandlot, looking for a sunny spot.

"Here!" she said. She lay down, her arms stiff at her sides, and wiggled down until the sand partly covered her. "It keeps the sun," she said.

Mitzi frowned uncertainly.

Ruthie pressed her cheek into the sand. "Oh, it's so warm. Come on, Mitz," she said.

Mitzi wiggled down next to Ruthie, her arms still covered with goose bumps. Overhead, white clouds raced in a blue sky. Mitzi smiled and turned to Ruthie.

"It *is* warm!"

"I told you," Ruthie said.

They lay snuggled into the sand, listening to the passing trolley cars and the sounds of boys shouting in the street.

"Know what?" Ruthie said.

"What?"

"I really hated you!"

"You did?" Mitzi said. "Why? Because of the invitation?"

"And because Shirl was my best friend."

"Well, I didn't think you were too nice, either!" Mitzi said.

Ruthie sat up, leaning on her elbow. *"After I stuck up for you?!"*

"Yeah . . . and then ditched me!"

"The way you put it," Ruthie said, feeling

guilty, "it doesn't sound very nice." She lay back down. "What do you do Saturdays?"

"Sometimes I help in the store," Mitzi said. "In Sacramento, if I had money, I went ice-skating."

"They have ice there?"

"Sure. In the ice rink."

"Oh, we have one, too. Down at the beach—Sutro's. I've never been. Is it hard?"

"No," Mitzi said. "It's easy. I could show you sometime."

"Goodie!" Ruthie had never gone inside Sutro's—a castle of white glass on a rock over-looking the ocean.

"What do *you* do Saturdays?" Mitzi asked.

"Oh . . . sometimes I just hang around here. Or go to the schoolyard and shoot baskets."

The wind rocked the telephone wires above them.

"I'll tell," Mitzi said.

"Tell what?"

"Who I love. But you have to promise to keep it a secret."

"I promise."

"You have to guess," Mitzi said. "I call him 'Mr. Mustache.' "

Ruthie thought through all the movie stars

with mustaches. As she named one after another Mitzi shook her head.

Finally Mitzi said, "I'll give you a hint: Robin Hood."

"Oh, him. He's always running around shouting and waving a sword." Heroes, Ruthie believed, should talk quietly and look deep into your eyes.

"I love him," Mitzi said. *"But don't tell."*

"Of course not," Ruthie said, happy to be trusted.

A foghorn blew.

Three planes roared overhead. All had stars.

"I think I havta go, Ruthie," Mitzi said, standing up, brushing off sand.

"It's early," Ruthie protested.

"I have a long ways," Mitzi said. "Know what I worry about sometimes?"

"What?"

"What if those girls—"

"Shirl and Barbara T.?"

Mitzi nodded. "What if they follow me home?"

"They won't," Ruthie said. "But what if? So what?"

Mitzi said nothing.

"What if they did?" Ruthie repeated.

Mitzi said, "Promise you won't ever tell? I mean really?"

Ruthie nodded.

"I don't live in this district."

"You don't?"

Mitzi shook her head. "I'm supposed to go to my old school in Japantown."

"*You* said you can change schools if you wanted!"

"I just said that. See, before the war started and everything, my father put down that we moved here. There's a lady in this district my uncle Joe knows. She said we could use her address. Ruthie, don't tell anyone!"

"Cross my heart and hope to die," Ruthie said.

They looked for their shoes. Ruthie hoped no one ever discovered Mitzi's secret.

"Ruthie!" Mitzi shouted. "You've got sand all over your back!"

"So do you!"

They took turns brushing each other off. They bent way over and shook their heads like rag mops.

"I can only go with you to the corner," Ruthie said when they were on the sidewalk, lacing up their shoes. "I'm supposed to stay on the block unless I get permission."

"That's OK," Mitzi said. "I had fun, Ruthie."

"Me, too."

Mitzi crossed the street. Ruthie called, "Tell your uncle Joe thanks for the chocolate."

Mitzi nodded and waved.

Ruthie waved back.

If you weren't in the schoolyard, it was OK to wave.

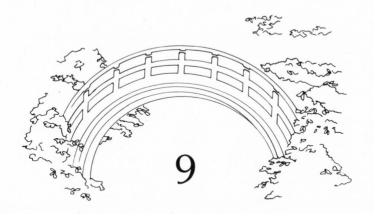

9

Almost Cocoa

Mitzi was going to play at Ruthie's house for the first time. It had been raining for a week, and Ruthie's mother said they could play inside after school. The girls were making plans over lunch in the cafeteria when Bev walked over.

"You didn't miss anything at Shirl's party," she said.

Good! Ruthie thought. She still felt bad about being left out.

"It rained," Bev said, "so there wasn't anything to do but sit in the Tea House."

"What did Trevino wear?" Ruthie asked.

"I was really surprised," Bev said. "She wore a nice dress and had ribbons in her hair and looked . . . really good!"

The bell rang and the girls collected their bags of marbles.

Ruthie could never figure out how it happened, but one day all the jump ropes were gone and everyone came to school with marbles. And the good thing about it, Ruthie told herself as she and the others kneeled on the cold basement floor, was that anyone could start a game. Nobody was in charge, unlike jump rope.

Other girls joined the game, then Shirl and Barbara T., who acted as if Ruthie and Mitzi weren't there.

Ruthie wished Shirl would stop being mad. She could make trouble if she wanted to.

Stop worrying, Ruthie told herself as she shot her cat's eye at Bev's whitey. Today Mitzi's coming over! Even if she has to go home first and change. Boy, is her mother ever strict!

When school let out, Ruthie told Mitzi the address again and they ran to their homes, jumping across puddles.

The doorbell rang just as Ruthie had finished stuffing the last of her comic books, magazines, board games, and dirty clothes into her closet.

Ruthie lived above her elderly landlords. Mrs. Rothstein was large, with gray hair piled on top of her head. She towered over frail Mr. Rothstein who almost never left his chair and his newspaper in the living room.

As Ruthie ran for the stairs, a knocking came from the floor. Oh, no! Ruthie rolled her eyes. She'd forgotten again. Mrs. Rothstein was reminding her about running on the hardwood floors. It disturbed Mr. Rothstein.

If you knew who was calling at Ruthie's, you could open the front door without going all the way downstairs by turning a metal handle built into the wall.

At the bend in the stairs Ruthie could see Mitzi's solemn face through the door curtain. She pulled the handle.

"Oh!" Mitzi said, surprised, when the door opened as if by magic.

"Come on in," Ruthie called down.

"Hey, that's fun," Mitzi said, climbing the stairs and shaking off the rain. "Can I try?"

While Mitzi worked the handle, Ruthie went outside and rang the bell.

"Is this where Mrs. Gotrocks lives?" Ruthie said in an old lady's voice when Mitzi worked the door handle.

"Oh, my dear, yes," Mitzi answered snootily from the stairs. "Are you the maid we ordered?"

"Maid!" Ruthie said indignantly. "I'm her rich sister who drinks. Tell her I'm here from Back East!"

Mitzi wanted Ruthie to go out again. This time Ruthie was a snarling Miss O'Connor. "'Is that Mitzi Fujimoto late again?'" she cackled. 'Thirty lashes and your mother, father, and uncle all have to come to school!'"

Mitzi doubled up laughing. "I want to be the visitor now," she said.

Standing on the stairs, Ruthie called, "Who's there?" and Mitzi shouted, "Mr. Dark Eyes' friend! He wants to marry you!"

"Today?" Ruthie moaned. "I don't have a thing to wear!"

As Mitzi climbed the stairs again, Ruthie said, "Come on, let's get something to eat."

She led the way down a long hall past airy rooms that didn't have much furniture.

"Is it always so quiet?" Mitzi said.

"My mother works."

"So does mine but when you live over a store, it's always noisy as anything!"

They popped popcorn in a pan on the stove, taking turns shaking it when their hands got tired.

"I wish we could make cocoa," Ruthie said. "The can got used up last week and there's no more in the stores."

"Ruthie," Mitzi said, "maybe we can make some."

"Some what?"

"Cocoa. Remember the story of Stone Soup?"

Ruthie shook her head.

"It's about this village where everyone is poor and hungry," Mitzi said. "A stranger comes to town and asks for food. 'We have none,' they say. He says, 'I've got this magic stone. It makes Stone Soup. Now boil up a pot of water.' So they do and he puts the stone in and tastes it. 'Not bad,' he says, 'but it could use a carrot.' Even though they're poor they have a carrot. He cuts it up. Then he says, 'Now an onion.' He cuts in an onion. 'A chicken wing,' he says, 'celery—' "

"—and pretty soon," said Ruthie, "they have soup! I remember that story! But we don't have a magic stone, Mitzi."

"We have milk, don't we?" Mitzi said. "The people in the village thought they didn't have things for soup."

"Mitzi, you're crazy!" Ruthie said. But she got milk and poured some into a pan, thinking happily how no one else she knew would do something crazy like this. She handed Mitzi a big wooden spoon.

"Now . . . what else?" Mitzi said stirring the pot over a low flame.

"Vanilla?"

"Vanilla!"

Ruthie poured in a teaspoon from the dark bottle.

The pot gave off a lovely smell.

"OK, what next?" Ruthie said.

"Ummm . . ." Mitzi said, thinking. "Cinnamon?"

"Yes!" Ruthie said. She shook the spice can into the pot until the milky surface was speckled brown and smelled like cookies.

They stirred and thought.

"Ruthie, you know what we forgot?" Mitzi said. "Sugar!"

Ruthie measured out two heaping teaspoons. "I hope this is enough," she said. "My mother will kill me if I use more."

The mixture was getting thicker.

"Let's taste," Mitzi said.

"It's too . . . white," said Ruthie, licking a spoon.

The morning coffee sat on the stove. Ruthie's mother made it by throwing fresh grounds on an open pot of water then straining it.

"Ever drink coffee?" Ruthie asked.

Mitzi shook her head.

"Me, neither," said Ruthie. They giggled as Ruthie dribbled in just enough to turn their milky mixture brown.

"Now," said Mitzi, stirring, "we have to think 'chocolate.' "

"Chocolate, chocolate," they thought as they stirred, concentrating on the memory of its sweet taste.

Finally they poured the hot mixture into cups. Taking their popcorn, they sat down at the table.

"It has a skin like cocoa," Ruthie said.

"It sort of smells like cocoa," Mitzi said.

They took a sip.

"It almost tastes like it," Ruthie said.

Mitzi agreed. "Almost Cocoa!" she said.

"Mitzi! We invented something: Almost Cocoa!" Ruthie said. "And you have a mustache!"

"So do you!"

"It must be fun to live over a store," Ruthie said when they had emptied their cups and wiped their mouths. "Do you get to work there?"

Mitzi nodded. "I put groceries on the shelves, and when my mother fixes dinner I work the cash register."

"With real money?" Ruthie was awed. It was

funny—Mitzi's mother seemed so strict but Ruthie couldn't imagine anyone else she knew being allowed to take the money in a real business.

"You can visit," Mitzi said. "Would your mother let you?"

"Sure," Ruthie said, wondering if she would.

Ruthie's bedroom was at the back of the house. They sat on her bed, a four-poster. Mitzi ran her hands down one of the four maple posts. Each had a top scored like a pineapple.

"This bed used to be my parents'," Ruthie said. "But when my daddy started at the ship-yards, my mother bought them a new bedroom set and I got this."

Mitzi wanted to see the new set so they went to Ruthie's parents' room. The furniture had straight lines.

"I like your four-poster better," Mitzi said back in Ruthie's room.

"Me, too. See, my mother likes new things but I like old."

"You, too? I *never* throw anything away," said Mitzi. "And my mother yells about that!"

"You, too?" Ruthie said, thinking of all the things she had crammed in the closet and under the bed that Mitzi might like to see.

They turned on their stomachs and looked at the gray line of ocean past the rooftops.

"I've never seen the ocean," Mitzi said, staring out the window.

"There it is."

"I mean up close."

Ruthie couldn't imagine it. From the time she could remember she was taken down to wade in the ice-cold surf.

"When we go ice-skating you'll see lots of it," Ruthie said. "Sutro's is over there—" She pointed past the window but all they could see was a gray watery strip. "I always think it's full of kings and queens dancing."

Suddenly the house rattled and shook.

"What's that?" Mitzi said, wide-eyed.

Ruthie laughed. "The B car. You know, the trolley. Now do you think it's quiet?"

Mitzi smiled a big smile, shaking her head. "I thought it was an earthquake!" she said.

"I like the trolley," Ruthie said. "When I'm here alone, it's like a friend going by. It's always there. All day and all night."

"In my old house in Sacramento," said Mitzi, "we could hear a rooster crow."

"I never heard a real one," Ruthie said. "Do they crow a lot?"

Mitzi laughed. "Every morning," she said. "I miss it now but my daddy says he doesn't. 'That rooster never knew when it was Sunday,' he says."

Ruthie laughed.

It was still drizzling, so Ruthie took out the old Sears catalog and showed Mitzi how she made paper dolls by cutting out people and then finding the things they needed that matched their size.

"Oh, let's do that," Mitzi said, turning the big pages.

They sat on the dining room floor under the table and cut out people, making up stories and acting them out.

Every time the trolley went by rattling the house, Mitzi would look up startled and Ruthie would laugh and Mitzi would wiggle her shoulders pretending to be all shaken up.

After an hour, Mitzi stood up. "I havta go," she said, making a long face.

Ruthie made a matching face. They agreed to meet at the lot the next day if it didn't rain—or at Ruthie's if it did.

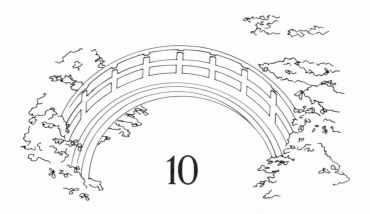

10

Treasures of the Drowned

That night as Ruthie was clearing the table, her mother said, "Honey, after this you and Mitzi will have to stay outside. Mrs. Rothstein complained about you running through the hall."

"She always complains," Ruthie grumbled. Still, she liked her landlady who wore a cameo pin in the center of her large bosoms and always chatted with Ruthie on the street.

Ruthie didn't mind staying outside but what about Almost Cocoa? She hadn't really told her mother about it. There was the problem of the rationed sugar they used plus the coffee they weren't supposed to drink.

"Can Mitzi and me come in just long enough to fix snacks?" Ruthie said. "We'll be quiet, I promise."

"I don't know," her mother said, frowning. "You always promise then forget."

"But I have to eat something," Ruthie said. "You don't want me to starve, do you?"

"Oh, all right. But be sure and clean up. I don't want to come home to dirty pots again, Ruthie Fox!"

Ruthie nodded happily.

The next day Ruthie and Mitzi whispered in Ruthie's kitchen after school as they fixed their snacks. They cleaned up and walked softly down the stairs and shut the door. In the lot they leaned against the backs of the billboards, digging their bare feet into the sand, munching warm popcorn, and sipping Almost Cocoa—out of the world's sight.

The day after, the fog was so thick that half a block away people were only shadows.

Ruthie and Mitzi ate in silence watching the fog drift over the sandlot.

A foghorn called mournfully.

"What do you want to play?" Mitzi said, almost whispering. "Starving Romanians?"

Ruthie shook her head. "Let's explore . . ." she said.

70

They walked around turning over torn sheets of paper and examining small objects. Ruthie was up near the sidewalk when Mitzi called from the other end.

"Ruthie!"

Mitzi was holding something shiny and small.

Ruthie ran up. It was a worn gold tube.

Mitzi pulled off the top and turned the base. A purple-red lipstick rose.

"Where did it come from?" Ruthie said.

Mitzi looked over the lot. "'Uh-oh' O'Connor said that once all this part of the city was under water."

"Treasure!"

"Yes!"

They kept looking at the lipstick, rolling the tube up and down. There was something fascinating about the bright fuchsia color—more purple than any they had seen.

"Mitzi," Ruthie said, staring at it, "I bet . . . this belonged to a lady who drowned."

Mitzi frowned.

"A long time ago."

A foghorn made its warning cry.

"Then what if . . ." Mitzi said, "she lost other things?"

"Yes!" Ruthie said.

They tore across the lot. They sorted through wax bread wrappers and crumpled cellophane; through pages torn from school notebooks and tangled kite string; they poked in between the soft spikes of the purple iceplant.

ZOOM! The roar of planes broke the quiet.

A boy shouted from the sidewalk. "There they go," he cried, "to get the Japs."

Mitzi's face went still.

"Hey," Ruthie called. "Hey, Mitzi, what do you think she was doing? When she drowned?"

Mitzi stared into the fog. "Going to see faraway lands."

Ruthie sat down. "I think," she said, squeezing sand between her toes, "I think she was going to meet someone."

"Her true love?" Mitzi said, joining Ruthie.

"When the ship crashed—"

"And all hands were lost!"

Suddenly Mitzi turned and reached into the iceplant. Her hand caught something tangled in the roots.

It was silver with shiny blue stones.

Ruthie gasped. "Her earring! Oh, Mitzi—you find everything!"

"You'll find something," Mitzi said. "You will, Ruthie."

Ruthie got up and poked around in the dark

places by the fences, digging deep into the sand until it changed from dry to wet. The fog was so thick you had to bend down close to see.

Suddenly Ruthie spotted something shiny.

"Mitzi!" she cried, holding a chain of tiny silver balls that slid back and forth on little metal rods.

"See," Mitzi said, running over. "Her silver chain!"

They both looked at it and at a rotted sink plug nearby and laughed. "Yes!" they said.

"Come on!" Ruthie cried, leading the race back to the billboards.

They lay the treasures out in a row on the sand: gold lipstick, blue earring, silver chain.

"Ruthie," Mitzi said.

"What?"

"Do you think he married someone else?"

"Who?"

"Her true love."

"Of course, Mitzi."

Mitzi's face fell.

"But Mitzi," Ruthie added, "he remembered her. Always. Like Miss Lewis."

Mitzi looked blank.

"My teacher. Her fiancé was killed. Just one week after Pearl Harbor. To a day. She'll never forget him."

73

"I havta go soon," Mitzi said, standing up. She looked at the treasures. "What'll we do with them?"

Ruthie thought. "Bury them?"

"But what if someone finds them?"

"Nobody but us plays here," Ruthie said. "Let's mark it."

As they dug a hole, Ruthie whispered, "Be careful. Barbara T. lives on this block. She might see."

Mitzi's small body stiffened.

"She never comes into the lot," Ruthie said assuringly. "She lives across the street and her mother wants her to stay on her side."

Mitzi didn't smile. "It's a secret," she said.

Ruthie nodded. "Hey—a club."

"No one knows but us," said Mitzi.

They covered the last of the treasures with sand and marked the spot with a triangular black rock.

"Clubs have names," said Mitzi.

They thought.

"What about 'The Treasure Trove'?" Mitzi said.

Ruthie shook her head. "The lady has to be in it," she said.

They thought.

"What about . . . 'The Drowned Lady's Treasure Trove Club'?" said Ruthie.

Mitzi made a face. "Too long!" Suddenly she said, "Hey—what about . . . 'Treasures of the Drowned'?"

"I like that!" Ruthie said. She said it slowly: "Treasures of the Drowned."

As if in answer, the foghorn's low call came again.

"Now we swear in blood!" Ruthie said.

"I don't like blood," said Mitzi.

"Come on, Mitz. It won't hurt," Ruthie said, digging up the earring and looking for a sharp spot on it. But Mitzi shook her head firmly, no.

"I know!" Ruthie said, taking the lipstick. She pulled up Mitzi's sleeve. High on her delicate shoulder she wrote: *T.D.* in tiny letters.

She handed the tube to Mitzi who did the same to her.

They examined their marks. The dark red-purple letters shone brightly against their skin.

Pulling their sleeves down, they buried the treasures again and marked the spot with the black rock.

"And we can't wash for—" said Ruthie.

"—a week!" Mitzi said, tying her shoes.

"I was going to say 'a month'!"

75

"Two weeks!" they agreed.

"Tomorrow?" Ruthie said, walking Mitzi to the corner.

"Tomorrow," Mitzi said.

As Ruthie watched Mitzi go, her shoulder suddenly itched. Very carefully, she rubbed around the spot that covered the secret letters, T.D.

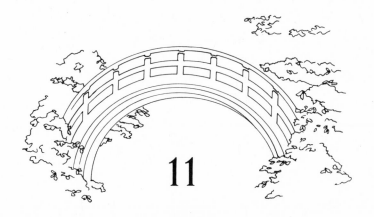

11

Curfew

A few weeks later, toward the end of February, Mitzi was invited to Ruthie's for dinner. For once her mother didn't make her go home first and change.

Ruthie's father had to work late so it was just Ruthie, her mother, and Mitzi at the dinner table.

"I feel like I already know you, Mitzi," Ruthie's mother said. "I've heard so much about you."

Mitzi smiled shyly and cut into her chop.

Ruthie looked back and forth from her

mother to Mitzi, excited that the two people who meant so much to her were finally meeting.

"Was it hard moving here from Sacramento?" Ruthie's mother asked.

"Sort of," Mitzi said, "but I like it now."

Ruthie smiled. Her mother was good at remembering things about people. Ruthie wished *she* could. It wasn't exactly that she forgot so much as she tended to say the first thing that popped into her head—which sometimes embarrassed everyone.

"Do you have brothers and sisters?" Ruthie's mother asked.

"Just one brother. He's overseas fighting."

"A brother?" Ruthie said. "Mitzi, you never told me!"

Mitzi gave her one-shoulder shrug. "Never thought about it," she said. "He joined up the day after Pearl Harbor."

"Do you write him?" Ruthie asked.

Mitzi laughed. "Ruthie—of course, what do you think?"

Ruthie didn't miss having brothers and sisters but it would be nice to say you had a big brother fighting overseas. Mitzi's mother must be old, Ruthie thought, to have a son that was at least eighteen.

Mitzi was telling Ruthie's mother the parts

of the city she had seen. "Golden Gate Park . . ."

"And the Tea Garden," Ruthie said.

"With the Moon Bridge," Mitzi said.

"Mitzi and I want to go there."

"It's hard, honey," Ruthie's mother said, "with gasoline rationed now."

The girls made comically sad faces.

"I've been to the Aquarium," Mitzi said.

"Ooo, it's spooky there," Ruthie said, "The fish stare at you." Ruthie made her eyes large.

Mitzi laughed. "You're crazy, Ruthie! The Aquarium's not scary!"

"Ooo," Ruthie said, making her voice go hollow. "Everything sounds like this."

"Ruthie, you loved the Aquarium when you were little," her mother said.

"I loved the seals, not the fish."

"I like the fish," Mitzi said. "There's all different colors and kinds."

"And they stare at you," Ruthie said in a spooky voice.

"Honey, you haven't been to the Aquarium in years," her mother said. "Don't pay any attention to her, Mitzi."

"I'm waiting for the war and rationing to be over," Ruthie said, wondering how long it would really be. Three months so far and it felt like a year.

Ruthie's mother served them dessert and poured herself coffee. She reached for the sugar bowl.

"I don't understand it," she said. "I've cut down to one teaspoon a cup but the sugar seems to disappear faster than ever. The coffee, too."

Mitzi and Ruthie ate their apple cobbler not daring to look at each other.

After they cleaned up, the girls went to Ruthie's room. Mitzi picked up the Monopoly set.

"Let's play this," she said.

"Oh . . ." Ruthie said, in a tired voice, "I played all Christmas vacation. With Shirl."

Mitzi thrust the box away as if it burned her hands.

"I hate that girl," she said.

Ruthie asked herself if she hated Shirl. What she felt was more like someone she once knew was dead. But the person who had taken her place . . . that person scared Ruthie.

The doorbell rang.

"Mitzi, it's your father," Ruthie's mother called from the door.

The girls ran to the stairs and leaned over the banister.

A thin man wearing work pants and a blue

80

denim shirt under a windbreaker smiled up at them.

"There you are!" he said to Mitzi.

"Oh, Daddy, do I have to go already?" Mitzi said.

"I'm afraid so," he said. "Get your things."

"Hi," Ruthie said, as Mitzi went to Ruthie's room.

"You must be Ruthie," said Mr. Fujimoto.

Ruthie nodded. She couldn't think of anything to say.

Mitzi's father looked as if he were trying to think of something also.

"It was very nice of you to have Mitzi," he said to Ruthie's mother.

"Oh, we enjoyed her!" Ruthie's mother said. "The girls are such good friends."

Ruthie walked down a few stairs. She could see a pickup truck waiting outside.

"Won't you come in?" Ruthie's mother asked.

"Thank you very much, Mrs. Fox," Mitzi's father said, "but my wife is waiting with dinner."

"This late? You haven't eaten yet?" Ruthie's mother said.

"No, we don't close till eight. Also, there's the curfew."

"Curfew?" said Ruthie's mother.

"We have to be back before nine or face arrest," Mr. Fujimoto said. He smiled but it was a polite smile without cheer.

"That's terrible," Ruthie's mother gasped.

"I agree," said Mitzi's father.

Could they really arrest people who hadn't done anything except stay outside? Ruthie wondered. She remembered that you could be arrested for keeping your lights on during a blackout, so maybe they could.

"I'm ready, Daddy," Mitzi said, running down the hall with her books and sweater.

"Shh—the Rothsteins!" Ruthie and her mother said together.

"Oh . . . I'm sorry," Mitzi said, her face turning red.

"Don't worry about it, honey," Ruthie's mother said, putting her arm around Mitzi and giving her a squeeze. "They're used to it—Ruthie never remembers."

Ruthie rolled her eyes.

"Thank you for dinner, Mrs. Fox," Mitzi said. "I had a really nice time."

"We enjoyed having you. Come again, dear," said Ruthie's mother.

We're all talking like people in a movie,

Ruthie thought. She felt silly saying things that weren't her own words.

Watching Mitzi get into the pickup truck, Ruthie thought how nice it would be to ride in one.

She waved good-bye, worrying about them missing the curfew. Would they really be arrested?

"What curfew?" Ruthie asked her mother as they closed the door and came up the stairs.

"So they're really enforcing it," her mother said.

"But it's not fair."

"I guess the government thinks if you make all the Japanese stay home at night," her mother said sarcastically, "the country's secrets are safe. Spies can't work during the day!"

"What if Mitzi's family wants to go to a movie?"

"It makes me so mad," her mother said, ignoring Ruthie's question. "You see—this is what happens when our politicians give in to the hysterical types. And they're the ones who shout the loudest!"

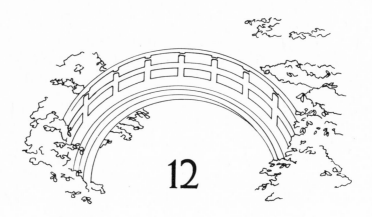

12

Sutro's-at-the-Beach

On a Saturday in March, Ruthie was waiting for Mitzi where the trolley stopped at her corner. After weeks of saying no, Mitzi's mother had finally agreed to let her off work to make the long trip to Sutro's-at-the-Beach. "Be sure and wear pants," Mitzi had warned Ruthie. "Or the ice will freeze your legs off."

Mitzi appeared in the distance wearing a knitted red hat with a tassel. As she came closer, Ruthie saw she was carrying white ice skates over her shoulder.

"I was afraid my mother was going to

change her mind!" Mitzi said. "I rushed out the door!"

"You have your own skates?" Ruthie asked. She'd never even skated before. She wished she had a hat like Mitzi's.

"I got them for my birthday," Mitzi said. "I wanted them for a long time. Here"—she handed Ruthie a pair of blue mittens—"in case you forgot."

"Thanks!" Ruthie said, putting them in her pocket. "I didn't forget—I don't have any. Mitzi, if you're real good I'm going to feel dumb."

"I'm not," she said. "Don't worry!"

They craned their necks for the trolley and looked up at the overcast sky.

"It's going to clear up," Ruthie said.

"Here it comes!" Mitzi cried, waving at the redwood-colored streetcar.

The girls boarded and sat in the outside section. They liked to watch the conductor making change as she rapidly flipped the levers of the metal coin holder at her waist. At each stop, she'd check the street for stragglers, then pull the cord that went *ding-dong* to signal the motorman to move on.

"I've never seen a woman conductor before," Ruthie whispered.

"Women are doing everything now," Mitzi said. "Like Bev's mother being a traffic cop."

"I love the B car," Ruthie said, the wind blowing her hair as they headed down the Anza hill. "It takes you everywhere: down to the beach and up to downtown—"

"How can downtown be up?" Mitzi said.

Ruthie shrugged. "I guess because you go up a hill to get there! But what I was saying before I was *so rudely* interrupted . . ." She pretended to frown.

Mitzi giggled.

". . . was," Ruthie continued, "it takes you everywhere: downtown where you can shop at the Emporium and City of Paris and go out to lunch with your mother and buy a gardenia for your lapel from the flower stands."

"Ooo, then I love the B car, too!" Mitzi said.

It was still overcast when they reached the end of the line. The girls walked with their heads bent against the wind under the rattling supports of the Big Dipper roller coaster. They crossed the highway and climbed a hill along the beach's sea wall until they came to a white building on a cliff with a white glass dome.

The girls passed the Cliff House, the restaurant next to Sutro's that shared the cliff, and entered a long drafty hall lined with stuffed monkeys in glass cages. It smelt musty.

Ruthie stared at the spooky moth-eaten chimpanzees and gorillas staring back through glass eyes. "What are they for?" she whispered.

Mitzi did her one-shoulder shrug and said, "Maybe they died in the zoo?"

Ruthie shivered and said, "Let's find the rink!"

They made their way through steamy crowds to the rental desk where Ruthie waited for her skates along with crowds of children and grown-ups.

She wanted beautiful white skates like Mitzi's but was handed black ones that were old and wrinkled.

"Rental skates are always black," Mitzi explained.

The girls laced up, and Ruthie put on Mitzi's blue mittens. Holding hands, they hobbled to the ice.

People of all ages and sizes were gliding smoothly around the rink. It didn't look too hard. But as soon as they were on the ice, Ruthie grabbed for the wooden side.

"Help!" she said.

"It's easy!" Mitzi told her. "Come on, I'll hold you. Don't look down."

At first Ruthie clung to Mitzi, but Mitzi showed her how they could cross arms and hold hands for better balance. Soon they were circling the rink with everyone else.

"Don't lean backward!" Mitzi reminded her. "If you think you're going to fall, lean forward!"

Breathing in the sharp icy air, Ruthie found herself magically sailing round with the other skaters to waltz music.

They became part of it all: the two big boys showing off, zigzagging through the crowd and making little circles round a trio of pretty girls who giggled; an old couple with arms crossed skating along effortlessly; a crowd of children from Chinatown who chattered to each other in Chinese and laughed whenever they fell down—which was often.

If she didn't think about it Ruthie found she could keep going, but once she stopped to marvel at the two of them gliding round and round, she would start to fall.

One time she pulled Mitzi on top of her.

"I'm sorry!" Ruthie wailed.

"It's OK!" Mitzi said with a big smile. "You have to fall. If you're afraid to, you never learn."

"How come *you* never fall?" Ruthie said.

"I used to. I used to all the time," Mitzi said.

After a while Ruthie wanted to rest. The

girls skated off the ice and stood at the side and watched.

A lady in a little blue skating dress with a matching cap was doing fancy turns alone in the very center. Ruthie couldn't believe anyone that good wasn't in the movies.

Looking at her white skates, Ruthie realized that Mitzi could probably do more than just circle the rink with her.

"Go on," she said, "you skate alone for a while."

"You sure?"

Ruthie nodded happily. She liked watching the people laughing and holding onto each other. She liked the special announcements: "Girls Only," or "Boys Only," or "Couples," or "Counterclockwise," and special games of tag and such that only the good skaters played.

Mitzi glided to the center. She started with little circles and turns just like the lady in blue, then went backward and forward with one leg in the air, and spun and glided and spun some more, the red tassel of her cap standing straight out.

And she said she wasn't any good! Ruthie thought, staring as Mitzi expertly pirouetted with one leg straight out, with a blank-faced look of someone concentrating, not in a show-off way at all. If Ruthie were that good, she wouldn't be able to keep from smiling, the way Shirl did when she made it to twenty-one in jump rope.

"Sure, you're terrible!" Ruthie teased when Mitzi skated off the rink. "You're better than the lady in blue!"

"I am not!" Mitzi protested with a happy glow.

"Just wait until we play basketball!" Ruthie said, grinning.

Ruthie returned her skates and felt strangely wobbly in her shoes again. The girls walked out past the spooky stuffed apes and over to the terrace alongside the Cliff House.

"Come here," Ruthie said, running to the rail at the edge.

Below them giant waves crashed angrily, climbing the rocks almost to where the girls stood. The terrace floor was wet with icy foam.

Mitzi stared fascinated.

"It's one of my secret places," Ruthie said over the roar. "Sometimes I come here and just look at it."

"All alone?" Mitzi said surprised.

"No. Sometimes Shirl and I came," Ruthie said. "But she always just wanted to go on the rides at Playland."

The girls stared into the lashing waves that battered the rocks with a thunderous noise.

"You can scream and can't even hear it," Ruthie said.

"Let's try."

"What if someone hears us?" Ruthie said, suddenly feeling silly.

"You said they can't."

Ruthie loved the way Mitzi seemed so proper but had more nerve than anyone she knew.

"Now!" Ruthie said.

The girls leaned into the waves and screamed. It was true—the crashing water drowned them out. But a huge wave answered by spraying their faces and hair. They stepped back, blinking and laughing.

They walked around to the sunny side. Seal Rocks jutted up from the sea just below them. Brown sea lions stretched their necks and honked and plunged into the water.

"You know," Ruthie said as Mitzi put a nickel in a viewing machine, "sometimes at night, when I think of the ocean, I get afraid."

"Why?" Mitzi asked as she steered the viewer from one end of the horizon to the other, past a gray battleship.

"Can you see the seals' faces?" Ruthie asked.

"No, the little cover is already coming down!"

"Oh, it's such a cheat!" Ruthie said angrily. "They don't give you any time at all."

"I saw part of a ship," Mitzi said, backing away as the metal plate dropped over the eyeholes.

"Oh, a ship," Ruthie said in a bored voice.

"I saw it up close!" Mitzi said.

"It's just like a toy one."

"Well, I've never seen one up close before and I want to," said Mitzi, suddenly angry. "You've done all these things, Ruthie, but I haven't."

"What things?" Ruthie said, surprised at Mitzi's anger. "You're the ice skater. I was falling all over the place."

"You know what things," Mitzi said, still angry. "Going downtown, seeing the ocean, knowing everyone at school, knowing which stairs to take. I'm always doing everything after everyone else!"

"You were *smiling* when you told me about the wrong stairs!" Ruthie said.

"Sometimes I smile when I feel dumb," Mitzi said, staring at the water.

"Well," Ruthie said after a minute. "OK, I shouldn't have said anything about the ship."

Mitzi didn't turn around. "It's OK," she said.

"It just seems dumb to see people jumping up and down shouting, 'I saw a ship!' when they look just like toy ones," Ruthie explained. "They're not pretty or anything."

Mitzi still didn't turn around.

"OK," Ruthie said. "Do we have another nickel?" she asked, feeling her pockets.

"Never mind," Mitzi said, turning at last and walking to the street. "They don't give you any time. Like you said—it's a cheat."

Ruthie followed her, wishing she had shut up and let Mitzi discover the disappointment of seeing ships up close for herself. Sometimes, she realized, you could be right and still end up feeling lousy.

"Why do you get afraid?" Mitzi asked as they headed down the hill, walking along the seawall. "At night—thinking of the ocean?"

"Sometimes," Ruthie said, looking at the pounding surf, "I start thinking—what if the waves just keep coming up? Just cover the streets and houses and come into my room?"

"But they always go out again," Mitzi said.

They stopped to lean against the sea wall.

"But why? I mean, what if once they didn't?"

"But they have to."

"Why? What makes them?"

93

Mitzi shook her head. "I don't know."

They walked on farther. The ocean filled the horizon as far as they could see.

The girls sat on the stone stairs in the wall to watch a barefoot lady on the beach who was throwing a stick to a little dog.

"Don't tell anyone," Ruthie said. "About what I said about being afraid at night. . . ."

"Ruthie," Mitzi said, looking hurt. "I wouldn't!"

"Okay . . . boy, look at those breakers!" Ruthie said. "They look like they're coming straight at us!"

"I think it's the moon," Mitzi said. "The moon makes them go out again."

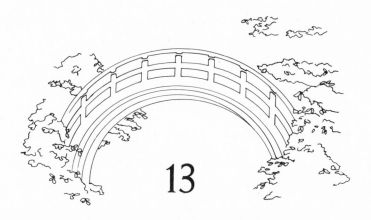

13

Loose Lips

The following week Ruthie and Mitzi were in the sandlot after school searching for more treasures, but they found only old PTA handouts and bits of string.

The sun had finally come out. Fleecy clouds floated in a bright blue sky.

Mitzi was looking up at the top of the billboards.

"Ever climb up?" she said.

"You mean all the way?" Ruthie asked.

When Mitzi nodded, Ruthie shook her head uncertainly.

"Let's do it," Mitzi said.

"Want to?" Ruthie said. It seemed awfully high.

In the corner where the two billboards met were short supporting beams like steps all the way to the top. Mitzi started up. Ruthie followed slowly.

"Hey, it's great up here!" Mitzi said when her head rose over the top.

"Wow!" Ruthie said, joining her.

In the clear spring air, they could see rows of white and pink houses sloping down to the beach with the green swath of Golden Gate Park sandwiched in between.

"Can you see the Tea Garden?" Ruthie asked.

They looked for the pagoda roof but the park was solid green—as if the trees had melted together.

Far below on the street, people scurried by.

A man in a hat carried a newspaper.

"Hey, mister!" Ruthie called. She and Mitzi laughed when he looked around.

"HOO HOO," Mitzi called to a woman in a scarf.

The woman turned, frowning.

The girls were laughing so hard they almost lost their footing.

"My mother would kill me if she could see me now," Ruthie said.

Two boys chased each other around the corner. One grabbed the other and they started wrestling.

"Bad boys!" Ruthie yelled.

The boys stopped and jumped up.

The girls ducked behind the sign, giggling with their hands over their mouths.

After a while they peered over the top again.

Now there was a woman carrying groceries.

"Lady—watch out!" Ruthie called.

The woman stopped and looked behind her.

"Ohmygosh, it's my mother!" Ruthie said, ducking down behind the billboard. "Do you think she saw me?"

"That's what you get for scaring her," Mitzi said, her shoulders shaking with laughter. She peeked over. "No, she's leaving. Ruthie—you should have seen your face!"

"Hey—it's not funny!" Ruthie said, trying not to laugh. But she began to break up, too.

All the way down—Ruthie couldn't look— they kept trying, but couldn't stop laughing.

At school they were planting Victory Gardens. On the last day of March, Miss Lewis' class stood by a patch of dirt in front of the school. While Ruthie's classmates pulled up weeds, Ruthie and Trevino waited to make beds for the seeds.

"I'm done!" Trevino said when Ruthie's row was only halfway finished.

"Good for you," Ruthie grumbled, patting the dirt smooth. Their class had radishes and she hated radishes. The only time she ate them was when her mother made them into roses for Thanksgiving.

As Bev sprinkled in the tiny seeds, Ruthie looked over to Mitzi's class at the next patch. String beans!

Mitzi sent Ruthie a superior smile.

After school Ruthie and Mitzi lay in the sandlot, their arms under their heads.

"Trevino always has to be first," Ruthie said. "Even digging dirt!"

"I got to use the sprinkling can," Mitzi said.

Ruthie rolled over to watch the paper boy go by on his bike. She loved to watch him pull the papers from the sack behind him and roll and toss them without ever holding on to the handlebars.

"When the war's over," Ruthie said, "I'm getting a bike."

"Me, too," Mitzi said. She got up to go. "Be careful tomorrow," she said.

"Why? What's tomorrow?"

"You'll see!" Mitzi said, laughing as she ran off.

The next day, two boys told Ruthie she had a spider on her back. One said he dropped a worm down her dress. Trevino tried to make her believe a doctor was coming to school and they'd all have to undress in the nurse's office.

After school, as Ruthie waited in the sandlot for Mitzi, she was thinking how nice it was that April Fool's was almost over.

Mitzi came running into the lot with a paper bag. Ruthie had asked to see the kimono doll again.

As Ruthie took it from the bag, she gently fingered the tiny paper fan and shiny hair ornaments.

"My mother will kill me if she finds out," Mitzi said.

They moved the black rock and dug up their treasures, renewing the faded T.D.'s on their arms. They arranged the earring, lipstick, chain, and kimono doll on the billboard's crossbar.

"What if someone sees her?" Mitzi said.

"Nobody ever comes back here," Ruthie said.

They went around to the sidewalk and drew

a hopscotch. The object you used to throw into the squares was called a *tor*—no one knew why. Ruthie's *tor* was a blue whistle from a Crackerjack box. Mitzi's was a button.

Mitzi was balanced on one leg, tilted forward to pick up her *tor* when Ruthie noticed that in place of the soldier waving good-bye, the sign now showed two workmen talking in a factory. Nearby, another with an evil smile listened. His eyes were slightly slanted.

"Your turn, Ruthie!" Mitzi called, from the hopscotch.

LOOSE LIPS SINK SHIPS the sign said above a ship's prow stuck into the air as the rest of it disappeared into the sea.

"Ruthie!"

Ruthie looked around.

"What are 'loose lips'?" Mitzi asked, reading the sign.

Bobbing her finger between her lips, Ruthie made her voice go shaky, "Luuu . . . uuuu . . . ssss . . . lippss."

Mitzi frowned. "Sink ships?"

"Does 'Uh-oh' O'Connor say what Miss Lewis does?" Ruthie put on a Southern accent. " 'Ruth-uh Fox, but-ton yo-ah lip.' "

"There she is!" someone yelled from across the street.

Ruthie and Mitzi's heads snapped around. Shirl and Barbara T.

Mitzi's face went dead.

"They won't come over," Ruthie whispered. "Barbara T. has to stay on her side of the block." Ruthie threw her *tor* into square 2. "My daddy's ships never sink," she said loudly.

"There's the Jap!" Shirl yelled as she and Barbara T. crossed the street.

Mitzi was backing up to the billboard.

"You better get outa here, Jap!" Shirl said, advancing with Barbara T. close behind.

"Who are you—the police?" Ruthie said.

Shirl pushed hair from her eyes. "Hey, Barbara T., didja hear about those Japs who got beat up?"

"Oh, 'April Fool,' " Ruthie said.

"Right near here, too!" Barbara T. said.

"One got killed," Shirl said. "He's one dead Jap now."

Ruthie looked at Mitzi. Her face said she believed every word.

"Cut that out!" Ruthie said, suddenly scared. "It's not funny."

Shirl came up to Mitzi who didn't blink.

"Get out if you know what's good for you."

They're serious, Ruthie told herself. This isn't an April Fool.

"I have as much right to be here as you," Mitzi said.

"Yeah," Ruthie said. "This lot is on *my* side of the block!"

Shirl shoved Mitzi. Mitzi pushed her back.

Little Mitzi actually shoved Shirl! Before Ruthie had time to think about it, Shirl pushed Mitzi hard. Mitzi stumbled but was still on her feet.

"Stop it!" Ruthie said, her heart pounding.

"I'm not a Jap!" Mitzi shouted. "My brother is fighting overseas!"

"For the Rising Sun," Shirl yelled.

"He is not! He joined up right after Pearl Harbor! He's over there saving your life!" Mitzi yelled.

"*My* father's over there while you're spying for the enemy!" Shirl said. "Like that." She pointed to the billboard.

"So you're blaming everyone else because your father has to fight?" Ruthie said.

Shirl turned around with wild eyes. "My father *wants* to fight! He's a soldier and proud of it!"

"We gotta get rid of the Japs here though!" yelled Barbara T.

Mitzi's eyes grew large. Shirl picked up a rock.

A rock? Ruthie couldn't believe it.

Slowly, Mitzi backed away. She turned and ran behind the billboard. Shirl ran after with Barbara T. following.

"Stop that!" Ruthie shouted, running after them.

Behind the billboard, Mitzi was climbing up the crossbar, past the treasures, higher than their heads.

Shirl aimed the rock.

Ruthie reached for Shirl's arm but Barbara T. grabbed Ruthie and held her.

"You better not, Shirl!" Ruthie said. Sweat was in her eyes and mouth as she struggled to get out of Barbara T.'s surprisingly strong grasp.

Ruthie looked around for help but no one could see them behind the billboards.

Mitzi was at the top. "Who do you think you are, anyway?" she called.

Shirl looked up angrily but Mitzi was beyond reach.

Ruthie stared, stunned at Shirl's actions.

Finally Ruthie broke loose. "Cut it out!" she said, pushing Barbara T. into the sand. She wanted to grab Shirl's arm but was afraid of that rock coming down on her own head.

Mitzi clung to the top of the billboard.

"Listen, Ruthie," Shirl said, narrowing her

eyes in a way that Ruthie used to think was so special. "You hang around the enemy, you get it, too."

Ruthie was so scared she couldn't even answer. It wasn't the fear of Shirl hitting her. Not even of her hitting Mitzi. What scared Ruthie now was the ugliness in Shirl's eyes.

Shirl let the rock drop. "They been warned," she said, brushing hair from her face. "Come on, Barbara T."

The two left the lot.

"They're gone, Mitzi," Ruthie called after a minute, her voice coming out cracked and strange.

Mitzi didn't move.

"They're gone," Ruthie said again.

After what seemed an hour, Mitzi began climbing down.

"Hey, Mitz," Ruthie said, smiling, "nobody ever pushed Shirl before!"

Mitzi didn't answer.

"Hey, they didn't even see our treasures!" Ruthie said, taking them down.

"I havta go," Mitzi said when she reached the ground.

"Listen, Mitz—they're just making that up. To sound big."

Mitzi looked at Ruthie. "No, it's true," she said. "It was in the papers. A man was beaten and another was killed. Just for walking down the street."

Ruthie felt sick. "But . . . you're just a kid. They won't do anything to you."

Mitzi moved the black marker rock and dug a hole.

"Aw, come on, Mitz," Ruthie said, kicking sand. "You gonna listen to those dummies?"

Mitzi buried the lipstick, the earring, and the chain.

"Mitz, did you see old Barbara T. down in the sand?"

Mitzi took her doll and dropped it in the hole.

Ruthie stared. *"Mitz, what are you doing?"*

Sand fell on the kimono. It fell on the shimmering hair ornaments and on the paper fan.

"Mitzi, are you crazy?" Ruthie said. "She's getting ruined!"

Mitzi covered everything with sand and marked the place with the black rock.

"Mitzi," Ruthie said, grabbing Mitzi's arm, "You can't bury your doll!"

Mitzi stood up and shook off Ruthie's grasp. She headed out of the lot with Ruthie following.

Ruthie wished she could make Mitzi talk.

"What about our club?" Ruthie called, forgetting it was supposed to be a secret.

Mitzi shrugged and kept walking.

Ruthie wasn't supposed to leave her block but she ran across the street and grabbed Mitzi's arm.

"Hey," she called, "you're acting like I was with them. Mitzi—remember how you asked if I could visit your store? What if I can? Tomorrow? Tell me the number again."

Tears came to Mitzi's eyes. "I shouldn't have come to this school!" she said. "My mother was afraid of this. Even *before* the war started!" She turned and kept walking.

Feeling sick, Ruthie watched her go. How could Mitzi lump her with those other two? Hadn't the time they'd spent together counted for anything?

Ruthie turned and started for home.

Suddenly from far away came the words, "GEary 6073."

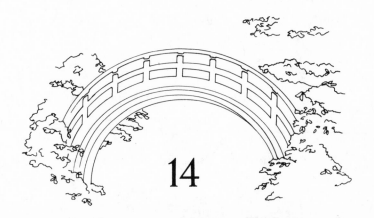

14

Kitchen Conference

"Honey, I don't want you to go."

"Mom-mee! You always let me visit friends. Why?"

Ruthie hadn't been able to wait until her mother had had her coffee and now she wanted to kick herself. The conversation wasn't going the way she'd planned.

Her mother was still in her black dress from work. She liked a cup of coffee in the kitchen before changing to start dinner. Ruthie had just finished telling her what had happened in the lot.

"That's horrible," her mother had said. "I

don't blame Mitzi for not wanting to come back.
I know she's your friend, honey—"

"My best friend."

"But . . ."

"What?"

"Oh . . . something . . . could happen," her
mother was saying now as she frowned and blew
on the steaming cup. She reached for the sugar
bowl and stopped. She'd already taken her limit
of one teaspoon.

"Like what? What could happen?" Ruthie
said. "Her mother will say it's OK. Please."

Sipping coffee, Ruthie's mother looked at
the ceiling. "It's just . . ."

"Just *what*?"

"Honey, give me a chance! If Mitzi didn't
live in Japantown, it would be fine." She took
another sip. Suddenly, she smiled. "I know! Ask
Mitzi to come here. Tomorrow's my day off
and—"

"Her mother will never let her," Ruthie said,
shaking her head, "after what happened."

"It's just . . . well—Oh, people are acting
crazy. You should hear the things they're saying
downtown."

"Like what?"

"Like . . . 'We should send them all back to
Tokyo.' 'They want us to lose. . . .' "

"It's not true!" Ruthie said.

"I know," her mother said. "But there are crazy people running around, honey. Stirring up trouble."

"I know that!"

"I don't mean kids, honey. I mean grown-ups, too."

"Mommy," Ruthie said quietly, "think how Mitzi will feel if I say no."

Her mother looked at her hard and sighed.

"Please call and say it's OK."

Ruthie's mother looked at the ceiling as if for an answer. "I want to let you but—oh, honey, Japantown is a long way from here. You girls are walking. Something . . . could happen."

"What? We'll be together."

Her mother took a second spoonful of sugar and stirred it into her coffee.

A key turned in the lock.

"You're a cheerful bunch," Ruthie's father said as he put down his paper and lunch pail. "What is it? Decimals or fractions?"

Ruthie's father liked to joke. It sometimes made him hard to talk to.

"Mommy says I can't visit Mitzi, and I promised," Ruthie said.

"She lives in Japantown, Hank," her mother said.

Ruthie's father took off his jacket and rolled up his sleeves.

Ruthie wanted to rush in but told herself: Don't put your two cents in . . . yet.

"Honey, look," Ruthie's father said to her mother, washing his hands. "Isn' it all this *thinking* something's going to happen that half the time *makes* it happen?"

Her mother sighed.

"You know," he said, "there was a guy down at the shipyard who got in a fight because some other guys were going around saying he was a spy. And why? Because he kept writing notes and stuffing them in his pocket. Turned out," he said, drying his hands on the dish towel, "his wife was having a baby and he was just trying to remember all he had to do. People are getting so crazy that Chinese are now carrying cards that say, 'I'm Chinese from Canton.' "

He shook his head. "And we call ourselves 'The City That Knows How.' "

Ruthie's mother didn't say anything.

Ruthie stared. She couldn't remember her father ever making such a long speech.

"Maggie," he said, pouring himself coffee, "what would you let Ruthie do normally?"

"I'd let her go."

"Then let her go."

"Hooray!" Ruthie shouted.

"I didn't say yes, did I?" her mother said, sharply.

Ruthie put on a serious face.

"Because, honey," her father said, "that's how things start. Let's say you tell Mitzi's mother that Ruthie can't go. Next thing you know, someone else hears it and tells *their* children to stay away from Japantown. Then the troublemakers go over to see what's up. And the *next* thing you know there *is* trouble!"

"Nothing's going to happen," Ruthie said, unable to keep still. "I'll be at Mitzi's. What can happen? Nothing. OK?"

She handed her mother a scrap of paper with Mitzi's number. "So just call and say—"

"I *know* what to say," her mother said, taking the paper. "But you can't go tomorrow."

"Why not?"

"Tomorrow's Thursday, my day off, and we have to get you shoes."

"Oh, no." Ruthie hated buying boring shoes. "The next day? Friday?"

Her mother sighed and went to phone.

"Hello?" Ruthie heard her say from the hall. "This is Ruthie's mother, Mrs. Fox. Is Mrs. Fujimoto there?"

Ruthie smiled at her father. Usually he left decisions about her to her mother. Boy! When he wanted to—he sure could talk!

Now in just two days she'd be visiting Japantown where Mitzi lived over a store.

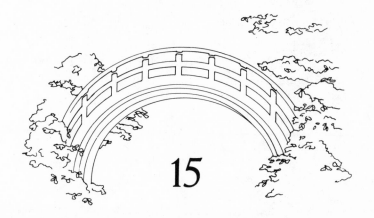

15

Japantown

"Step on a crack,
Break your mother's back.
Step on a line,
Break your mother's spine."

"You stepped on a crack, Ruthie!"
"Did not!" Ruthie answered, hopping ahead
in her new brown-ugly shoes. At the shoe store
yesterday there had been nothing to choose from:
brown-uglies or uglier black.

"Shortages," her mother had said, shaking her head in the store. "Honey, we're lucky to get *anything*."

"Hey, Mitz—" Ruthie started to say when she noticed the boys who spotted planes behind them.

Looking at Mitzi, the boys nudged each other.

Mitzi saw them, too.

Staring straight ahead, the girls crossed the street.

What if they followed us all the way, Ruthie was thinking, and found out Mitzi lived outside the district?

Ruthie forgot about the boys when suddenly all the signs had Japanese characters and the streets were filled with people. She had passed through Japantown on the trolley but never on foot. In the air were strange smells that made her feel shy: a mixture of vinegar and fish and food cooking. She kept turning her head to see everything and grabbing Mitzi's arm in excitement.

"Mitzi, can you read that?" Ruthie asked, pointing to a narrow sign with characters running from top to bottom. Next to it English words said, NISEI GRILL.

"Nisei Grill," Mitzi said.

"Mitzi!" Ruthie said. "I can read that!"

114

"Well, that's what the characters say, too!" Mitzi said.

In the Nisei Grill's window a neon sign flashed: DAY-NIGHT.

"I only know a few words," Mitzi said. "See that?" She pointed across the street to a wiggly line crossed with a dagger next to a huge paper fish. "That means 'lucky.' "

Next to the paper fish, paper birds in brilliant colors rode the wind. Ruthie thought she'd never seen anything more beautiful.

"What are they, Mitzi?"

"Kites."

"Kites!" Ruthie wanted to stay and watch the floating kites, but Mitzi pulled her on.

They passed vegetables that looked like fish and dried fish that looked like paper; food cut to resemble flowers and flowers that looked like paintings. Sometimes the smells from the vegetables made Ruthie feel sick and then she'd turn and see a delicate spray of spring flowers and want to stay.

In front of the Nippon Five-and-Dime a man sweeping waved to Mitzi, who waved back. HALF PRICE SALE! said a sign in his window next to the model airplanes and pink baby dolls.

A tiny old lady in a kimono bent nearly double with a baby strapped on her back ran along past them in quick steps as Mitzi turned into Joe's Groceries.

"How can an old lady have a baby?" Ruthie said but Mitzi was pulling her to the counter. The woman behind it said "Mitsuko!" and began nervously folding a newspaper covered with Japanese characters.

Ruthie guessed this must be Mitzi's mother.

"*Mitzi,* Mother!" a man corrected from the vegetable bins.

"That's my real name," Mitzi said, making a face.

"It's not bad," Ruthie said. "It's better than *Ruth.* Ever try saying 'Rooth' and looking *happy?*"

"*Mitzi,*" said the woman at the counter, smiling and nervously smoothing her paper.

"This is Ruthie, Mother," Mitzi said. "Ruthie, this is my mother."

Mitzi's mother was much older than Ruthie's. Her hair was gray and pulled back in a bun and she looked troubled. She didn't wear lipstick like Ruthie's mother, and Ruthie thought that even her mother's black saleslady dress was nicer than this plain brown dress Mitzi's mother wore under an old cardigan sweater. It was hard to think of Mitzi, with her big smile and small, pretty ways, coming from this lady.

116

"I talk to your mother on the phone," Mitzi's mother said.

Ruthie could see that her mother's speech embarrassed Mitzi, so Ruthie acted as if she didn't notice.

"It's a nice store," she said.

Mrs. Fujimoto made a little bow. "I'm glad you come," she replied.

"Me, too," Ruthie said, smiling and looking around.

Behind the counter were stacks of tiny boxes of all shapes, covered with writing and many with beautiful pictures of mountains and lakes and old mandarins with long mustaches.

"I thought mandarins were Chinese," Ruthie said to Mitzi.

"They are," Mitzi said. "It's hard to get anything from overseas now. We just take whatever we can get."

Around the store, cans bearing familiar labels like Del Monte Peaches sat next to foreign ones showing pictures of spidery-looking foods in unfoodlike colors of gray and pink.

"Come on," Mitzi said, pulling her to the bins of fresh fruits and vegetables where Mitzi's father and another man in grocers' aprons worked.

Ruthie remembered Mitzi's father from the day he picked Mitzi up. He was lean like a young man and frowned as he worked, but the shorter one, who was rounder, smiled at the girls over his shoulder as he trimmed lettuce.

"Daddy," Mitzi said, "remember Ruthie?"

As if waking from a deep trance, her father suddenly smiled. "Of course," he said. "How are you, Ruthie?"

"Fine, thanks," she said.

"And this is Uncle Joe," Mitzi said, pointing to the shorter man. "He's Mr. Fujimoto, too."

"Hello, Mr. Fuji . . . mo . . . to," Ruthie replied, getting her tongue around it.

"Just call me Uncle Joe, Ruthie," said Mitzi's uncle. "Everybody does."

"So you made the long walk!" said Mitzi's father.

"It wasn't so long," Ruthie answered. "I like all the shops. Are you brothers?" When they nodded, she said, "You don't look it."

The men laughed though Ruthie hadn't meant to make a joke.

"You're the one who gave us Hershey bars," Ruthie said to Uncle Joe.

"You liked them?" He turned to the bins of fruit and selected two red apples. "How about these today?"

"Ruthie likes chocolate, Uncle Joe," Mitzi said.

Uncle Joe shook his head. "It's very hard to get now. It all goes to the soldiers."

Ruthie nodded. "Like nice shoes," she said looking down at the brown-uglies.

Taking the apples, the girls headed up the stairs at the rear. An apple wasn't chocolate, Ruthie thought, but it *was* something she knew.

Mitzi's mother was calling. "Mitsuko!"

"*Mitzi*, Mommy!" Mitzi said, making a face over the banister.

"You have homework?" her mother said.

"Mother, Ruthie came here to *play*."

"That's OK," Ruthie said, not wanting to upset Mitzi's nervous mother. "We'll do it fast."

A customer came in. She went over to Mrs. Fujimoto and the two ladies began frowning and speaking rapidly in Japanese.

Ruthie wondered, as she followed Mitzi up the stairs and down a hall, do people smile talking English and frown speaking Japanese?

Mitzi's room was like Ruthie's: a bed, a dresser, old dolls and souvenirs. It felt comfortable.

Throwing their books on the bed, the girls collapsed.

"Can you just take whatever you want to eat

119

and not pay?" Ruthie asked, untying the brown-uglies.

Mitzi nodded.

"You're so lucky," Ruthie said, kicking off the stiff shoes as Mitzi undid hers.

Lying on their stomachs with their legs crossed in the air, they started their homework, biting into the apples.

"You have the same math book I do!" Ruthie said, looking at her problem, then at Mitzi's, but Mitzi was on a different page.

"I wonder who thought up fractions anyway," Ruthie said, laying down her pencil. She wandered around Mitzi's room.

Mitzi took a bite and started another problem.

"Does the store belong to you?" Ruthie asked, looking over photographs on Mitzi's dresser.

"No, it's Uncle Joe's. See, my daddy was going to get his own store when we came here from Sacramento. Then Pearl Harbor came. And things got confused."

Ruthie nodded. The war had changed everything. Sometimes it was exciting, like in the movies where our side always won.

"My brother was going to help, too, and then he joined the army."

Ruthie's eyes went to the photograph on the dresser of young men in uniform with their arms around each other's shoulders. All were Japanese.

She carried the picture to the bed. "Which one?"

Mitzi pointed to a man with a big smile like hers.

"What's his name?"

"Sab."

"How come they're all Japanese?"

"Ruthie, they're Americans!" Mitzi said.

"Oh, Mitzi, I know that!" Ruthie said. "Stop being so touchy."

"You mean *nisei*," said Mitzi, "that means 'second generation'—first generation born here. Except my father *was* born here so Sab and I are *sansei*. My mother is *issei*—she *came* here."

Ruthie was totally confused. "Mitzi, all I want to know is how come they're all . . . 'neezi'?"

Mitzi nearly fell off the bed laughing. " 'Nih-say,' Ruthie!" She stopped and thought. "I don't know . . . friends, I guess."

"Where's Sab now?"

"Can't tell. Military secret."

"Oh, Mitzi, I wish I knew a military secret," Ruthie said, carefully putting back the picture. "Do you like him?"

"He's OK. He kisses girls."

"How do you know?" Ruthie ran to the bed.

Mitzi smiled. "I watched."

"Mitzi! What did they do?"

"Oh, they just closed their eyes and kept . . . you know."

"Like in the movies?"

"And Sab's hands kept going round and round on her back and when he'd move them, she'd grab them and then he'd get free and move them again."

Ruthie sat up in bed. "He did?"

"I think he wanted to tickle her."

The girls looked at each other out of the corners of their eyes and started giggling. They collapsed on the bed.

When Ruthie couldn't laugh anymore, she said, "I'm sick of this math," though she hadn't done any. She wandered over to the window. Those boys—the plane spotters—were out front! What were they doing over here anyway?

Suddenly she thought of something.

"Did your mother ask where your doll was?"

"She didn't notice."

"Mitz, I don't like thinking of her down in that dark hole."

Mitzi shrugged.

Ruthie felt uneasy. "Mitz—what if someone takes her?"

"She's a Japanese doll. No one would want her."

Ruthie suddenly felt sad. "I would," she said.

"Then she's yours."

"But won't your mother get mad? The doll's so fancy."

Mitzi closed her book. "My mother's thinking about other stuff now." She put her pencil down. "Sometimes I don't want to grow up. Grown-ups always worry."

"Yeah, but they get to do good things, too," Ruthie said, wandering around the room. "Like going to parties at night and wearing their hair up."

Suddenly Mitzi said, "I wish right now we were ice-skating at Sutro's."

"My feet go inside out."

"You just need practice."

"I wish I could skate like you," Ruthie said.

"Ruthie, you want to do everything!" Mitzi laughed.

"That's 'cause I'm an only child. I have to do all the things my brothers and sisters would do if I had them."

"Who said?"

Ruthie shrugged with one shoulder like Mitzi. "Nobody. I just do. Mitzi—how come your mother talks with an accent but your father doesn't?"

"I told you! He was born here but she came from the old country. She never lets me do *anything*."

"She had a funny look when we came in, Mitz."

"Oh, all this stuff—you know, people from Japantown getting beaten up—makes her nervous. She's just tired," Mitzi said, finishing her apple. "She has to stand at that cash register all day. And sometimes nights. I'm never going to work in a store. When I'm grown up, I'm going to sing for the soldiers."

"I thought you were going to be an ice skater."

"I am. A singing ice skater."

"Ohhh," said Ruthie, skating around the room, twirling and singing, "la la la," in a high voice. "I'm Mitzi-the-singing-ice-skater-r-r-r---"

"Stop!" Mitzi squealed.

"And I sing for the soldiers and sai-lors!" Ruthie sang.

"Not sailors! We're *army*!" Mitzi screamed as she grabbed Ruthie around the waist and pulled her on the bed. Ruthie fell backward, arms straight out, laughing.

"And I . . ." Ruthie started to sing between giggles when Mitzi suddenly shushed her.

"What's the matter?" Ruthie whispered.

"Someone's coming."

They listened. They heard men's voices.

"It's Daddy and Uncle Joe," Mitzi whispered.

"Why are we whispering?" Ruthie said. "They live here, don't they?"

"*Ssh!*" Mitzi said. "Yes, but they never come up. Until late." She crept toward the door.

The men's voices were raised. It sounded like an argument.

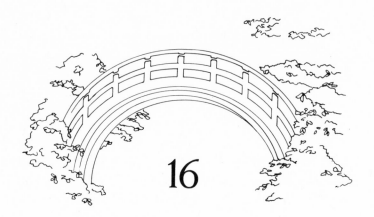

16

Something Shatters

"Tom, what are you doing?" they heard Uncle Joe say. "We should be downstairs taking inventory."

Mitzi signaled to Ruthie to keep still as she tiptoed out the door. Ruthie peered past Mitzi's head.

"We expected it, didn't we?" Uncle Joe said.

In the hallway, Mitzi's father was quickly walking to the back of the apartment, while his brother, on shorter legs, hurried to keep up.

"Did you hear about the Nisei Grill?" Mitzi's

father said, without turning around. "He sold it for *half* what it's worth."

Uncle Joe nodded to his brother's back. "Someone made me an offer today. It was so low, I thought they were kidding."

The men turned into a room down the hall. Mitzi and Ruthie quietly followed.

They heard the rustling of a box being opened and Uncle Joe's voice loud, half laughing, saying, "Tom—are you serious?"

The girls peeked into the room.

Ruthie guessed it was Mitzi's parents' room. There was an old-fashioned four-poster bed and pictures of babies on the wall. On the white chenille bedspread lay a dusty clothes box and from it, Mitzi's father was taking a brown jacket.

"When we go," he said, "I'm wearing this."

He buttoned an old army tunic over his grocer's apron.

"Tom! You're crazy!" Uncle Joe said. "From the First World War!"

Mitzi laughed, forgetting she and Ruthie were eavesdropping.

The men turned, her father with a scowl.

"Daddy!" she said, "you look funny!"

"Mitzi, go back to your room," he said sharply.

Uncle Joe smiled at the girls. "Your father's

remembering the old days," he said to Mitzi. He looked at his brother. "The old days are gone, Tom."

Something was wrong, Ruthie could tell—but what?

"Come on, Mitzi," she said, gently pulling her friend's arm.

"Mitzi," her father said, "we're busy now."

Mitzi nodded and let Ruthie pull her away. In the hall she said, "I think my daddy wants to join up."

Ruthie shook her head. "They won't take him. Only men with no children."

Suddenly they heard Uncle Joe's voice raised, "Tom, sometimes we don't understand but . . . we accept."

"My son is fighting overseas for the only country I've ever known," Mitzi's father answered. "I obey my government, Joe, but my heart . . . does not accept."

Something in his voice made Ruthie feel tingly.

"See, Ruthie," Mitzi said, "he wants to—"

CRASH! From downstairs came the sound of glass shattering.

Someone screamed.

The two men shot past the girls and raced down the stairs.

Ruthie and Mitzi, still in their stockinged feet, ran after them.

"Oh!" Mitzi cried, when they were in the store.

A crowd stood in front of Joe's Groceries. One window now had a large jagged hole. Pieces of glass lay over the stacks of bananas and apples in the front window. On the floor was a big rock.

Ruthie gasped.

Mitzi's mother at the cash register had her hands over her mouth. She motioned Mitzi to stay back but the girls followed the two men to the window. Mitzi's mother shouted at her.

Uncle Joe went to the open doorway and looked into the crowd. People were talking rapidly in English and Japanese, their faces angry and afraid.

Mitzi's father picked up the rock.

While Mitzi's mother called, "Girls, come back!" they followed Uncle Joe outside.

The plane spotters were running away.

"I know those boys," Ruthie said. "They're at our school!"

Farther down the street, she could see other boys. One was a flag bearer—every morning he marched with the flag for the Pledge of Allegiance. They were all sixth graders.

"Them, too!" she said.

She looked at Mitzi but Mitzi was staring with blank eyes.

"Uncle Joe," Ruthie said, "I know those boys."

"Ruthie, Mitzi," he said, "go back, please."

Mitzi's mother was calling to her in Japanese.

"It's just boys," Uncle Joe said, shutting the door.

Mitzi's father frowned, his dark eyes surveying the damage. "Don't you wish, Joe," he said. "Don't you wish it was 'just boys'? Just be glad no one was standing there."

Ruthie ran to the cash register. "Mrs. Fujimoto, I know those boys. I can report them. I know their teachers."

Mrs. Fujimoto shook her head. "Thank you, Ruthie, no."

"But it's wrong," Ruthie said, turning to Mitzi's father. "They know it's wrong."

Mitzi seemed to wake up. She ran over to Ruthie.

"Don't say anything in school, Ruthie, please."

Ruthie saw Mitzi's parents exchange a look. What was going on?

"Mitzi," Ruthie tried again, "come on, those boys are *awful*. Someone should tell."

130

"No!" Mitzi shouted.

Outside the crowd was still there, pointing to the hole, talking loudly.

"Ruthie," said Mr. Fujimoto, "it's not a school problem. I think you'd better go home. To be safe."

"Yes," Mrs. Fujimoto said. "I tell your mother I send you in time."

Ruthie nodded and went for her things. When she returned downstairs, Uncle Joe said, "Ruthie, we appreciate your help. We do."

"Oh, yes, yes," said Mrs. Fujimoto. "Thank you."

Ruthie turned to Mitzi. "Tomorrow? At the schoolyard?" The next day was Saturday.

"Mitzi has to help here," her mother said.

Mitzi looked sadly at Ruthie.

"See you Monday?" Ruthie said. "At the billboards?"

Mitzi nodded. "Good-bye, Ruthie," she said.

Ruthie pushed through the crowd in front of Joe's Groceries, hugging her books.

Even though it wasn't five yet, shops were closing. For the first time Ruthie noticed all the HALF PRICE SALE signs in the windows. At the kite store, a man was pulling down the shades and taking down all the kites.

Ruthie wanted to talk to her parents, to tell

them how strange and crazy everything suddenly was.

If she could just tell someone about those boys, she thought, passing through the emptying streets, then everything would be all right again.

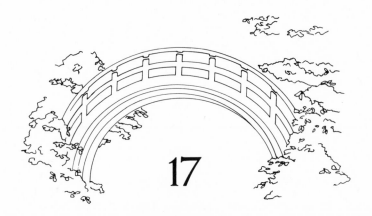

17

Blackout

As Ruthie raced up her front stairs, the wail of the air-raid siren cut through the evening chill.

"Mommy!" she called, slamming the door, but there was no sign of her mother. Dropping her books, she turned a light on, then remembering the air raid, turned it off again.

A door opened—her father was coming up the stairs two at a time.

"Mommy's not home yet!" Ruthie called over the wailing siren.

"Air raid!" her father said, dropping his lunch pail and rushing to the clothes closet.

Ruthie ran after him. "Daddy, at Mitzi's store today—"

"No time now, Ruthie," he said. "Got to patrol."

While the siren screamed *"Wah, wah, wah!"* Ruthie helped her father slip the air-raid warden's arm band over his jacket sleeve and, as he buckled the helmet, she handed him the flashlight and billyclub.

"They threw a rock at Uncle Joe's window," Ruthie blurted out.

"Oh, lord, no! Was anyone hurt?"

Ruthie shook her head.

"What's the matter with people, anyhow?" her father said. "We'll talk about it later, Cookie." He headed down the stairs and called up, "Ruthie, you'd better go down to the Rothsteins."

"I'm OK here," she said. She didn't want to talk to anybody now.

"Your mother must still be downtown," her father called from the stairs. "She'll have to stay in a shelter until the all-clear sounds."

"I know what to do!" Ruthie called back. " 'Bye, Daddy."

Ruthie found the fat candle saved for blackouts and lit it and placed it on the kitchen table along with the big padded cigar box that was kept in the hall closet.

She went from window to window carefully pulling down the regular shades and then the special coal-black shades that come down on top of them. All light had to be sealed out from enemy planes.

Usually Ruthie loved blackouts—the private feeling of being alone with her mother as they pored through the cigar box looking through old buttons and broken pieces of jewelry for enough cards to make a deck. Ruthie loved the pirate girl embossed on the cover with her big earring and head scarf and torn skirt who stood with one foot on a rock and seemed to speak of carefree adventure. In the strange darkness and city silence Ruthie and her mother would play gin rummy while her mother's diamond ring threw off a wild light.

But now as Ruthie sat alone at the kitchen table and counted out a deck of cards, everything seemed to have stopped still.

She lay seven down in a row and thought, In the whole apartment nothing is moving except my hand.

The room was lost in blackness except for the little space around the table that the candle's glow reached.

I'll call Mitzi, she thought. Then she remembered that only emergency calls were allowed.

Feeling very alone, Ruthie ran to a black-shaded window. She stepped between the window and the shade, reassured by the sight of her father's flashlight making a path up the block, checking that all lights were out.

She let the shade fall back, and returned to the kitchen by feel until she saw the candlelight. Sitting down, Ruthie thought about Mitzi's father trying on his old uniform, and the rock, and the shouting. Something bad was happening.

In the flickering candlelight, she lay the red queen on the black king with a trembling hand.

This is war, she told herself. Everyone has to do his part. Wasn't her father outside doing his? So I've got to do mine, too, and not be a baby.

Suddenly Ruthie felt exhausted. She put her head down on the table.

"Ruthie—!"

Ruthie opened her eyes. Her mother was gently shaking her.

The blackout shades were gone. Her father was at the stove making coffee. Ruthie blinked at the bright lights.

They were all safe! Ruthie threw her arms

around her mother and buried her face in her warm coat.

"You OK, honey?" her mother said. "I was stuck down in a shelter for the whole air raid! I worried about you! If I hadn't waited on that last customer . . . !" Her mother said again, "You OK?"

Ruthie nodded. Her mother touched her shoulder. "Ruthie," she said, "something's happened . . . in Japantown."

"I *know*! Those boys—from school—threw this rock—"

"That was terrible, honey! Daddy told me, but I meant . . . something else. Didn't Mitzi, didn't her mother . . . say anything?"

"About what?"

Her parents looked at each other. Now what was the matter with *them*?

"It's in the news," her father said. "Everyone in Japantown, Cookie. They have to report downtown."

"For duty? Because Mr. Fujimoto—that's Mitzi's father—except Uncle Joe is Mr. Fujimoto, too—was putting on his old uniform! But Uncle Joe told him he was crazy!"

"Hank, we don't know for sure," Ruthie's mother said. "I don't mean about reporting, I mean . . ."

"Maggie," he said, "the notices went up."

"But you hear one thing one day and another the next, Hank. I read the papers, too, but no one seems to know what's happening."

"I just don't think you should get Ruthie's hopes up," he said.

"My hopes aren't up," Ruthie said, not knowing what they were talking about.

"If I knew *what* to tell her, I would!" Ruthie's mother said.

"Cookie," said her father, "it looks like your friend will be leaving."

"Mitzi? No!" Ruthie said. "She would have said."

"Maybe she didn't know herself, honey," said her mother. Turning to Ruthie's father, she said, "I mean, *where* are they supposed to be going? Try and find that in the paper!"

He nodded. "What gets me," he said, "is these people who go around saying, 'It's for their own safety.' Sure, when kids start throwing rocks, it's not safe anymore, but—"

"—what are police for?" Ruthie's mother said, finishing his sentence.

"Mitzi isn't moving," said Ruthie. "Uncle Joe has his store. And she lives over it. So how could they move?"

"Ruthie," said her father, shaking his head, "when the government says 'do something' . . ."

Ruthie didn't feel like arguing. She put her head down on the table. Mitzi was meeting her after school Monday. In three days.

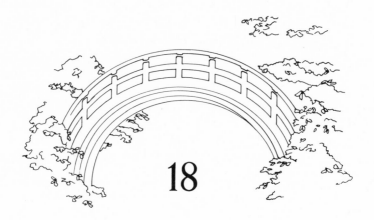

18

One, Two, Button
My Shoe

Saturday morning Ruthie was in the schoolyard at the baseline shooting baskets, her head buzzing with the sounds from the day before: glass shattering and people crying out and feet running.

Trying to make the sounds go away, she bounced the ball hard but when she took aim she saw—not the basket—but Shirl coming into the sandlot again, yelling and picking up that rock.

Ruthie dribbled the ball and ran with it,

shooting at one basket then the other, trying to push out the noises and pictures of the days before.

With relief, she saw Trevino come into the yard, pushing up the sleeves of her big sloppy sweater, hopping on one foot then another.

"Wanna shoot a few?" Ruthie said.

"Sure," Trevino said, "give it here."

She always has to be first, Ruthie thought, but she threw the ball. Trevino made a big show of dribbling and shooting. Her shot went in.

They decided each could shoot from the throw line until she missed.

Trevino made three in a row. As she aimed again, she stepped over the line.

"Over the line!" Ruthie called.

"The ball's still in my hands," Trevino argued.

Ruthie stared through the fence at the street not caring. She wanted to tell someone about what had happened at the store, but Mitzi made her promise not to.

Monday morning Ruthie looked for Mitzi when the classes went out to water and weed their Victory Gardens. Tiny flat radish leaves were poking up in straight rows in Miss Lewis' plot. Ruthie looked over excitedly at "Uh-oh's" patch to tell Mitzi but everyone was crowded around. Ruthie could only see Barbara T. waving a watering can over the sidewalk.

At recess and lunch Ruthie didn't see Mitzi. Maybe her mother was keeping her home.

After school, still in her school clothes, Ruthie hurried from her apartment to the sandlot, her house key bouncing lightly against her chest. She was supposed to change but she was afraid of missing Mitzi. Even if she hadn't come to school, Ruthie knew she'd keep her promise to meet in the lot.

Glaring up at the "Loose Lips" sign, Ruthie ran behind the billboards. She hummed to herself as she unfolded her surprise: two new pictures—Mr. Mustache in a pilot's uniform and Mr. Dark Eyes in a navy officer's. Ruthie hung them on crossbar nails.

Where was Mitzi?

Kneeling down, Ruthie watched passing feet through the crosshatch slats.

A dog sniffed around. An old woman with a cane tapped by.

Ruthie dribbled sand through her fingers. Maybe Mitzi's mother hadn't let her out, after all.

Ruthie thought of digging up the treasures. She hated to think of the silk kimono and paper fan covered with dirt but maybe it was better to leave them. People were acting so crazy.

Someone was coming!

Ruthie peered through the crosshatch. A girl's legs! Ruthie ran around to the street.

Barbara T. Unwinding a jump rope.

"One, two, button my shoe," Barbara T. chanted. "Shirl can't come out today. She's being punished for talking back."

Good, thought Ruthie.

"I bet I know who you're waiting for, Mitzi-the- —"

Ruthie glared and Barbara T. closed her mouth.

"Three, four, shut the door," she sang. "She's not coming."

"Like ducks," said Ruthie.

"Five, six, pick up sticks. I know 'cause I'm in her class."

Mad at herself for even talking to Barbara T., Ruthie asked, "Was she there today?"

"Nope."

"Then she's sick," said Ruthie. "Her mother wouldn't let her stay home for nothing."

"She's not sick. She's gone. For good!"

She's making that up, Ruthie thought, heading to the corner to wait for Mitzi.

"She's never coming! We got rid of them."

Ruthie turned around. *What?*

"The Japs! For good!"

"You're lying, Barbara T.!"

"Ask Miss O'Connor!"

"I don't believe you!" Ruthie said.

Ruthie wanted to run, to ask someone, then she remembered her pictures hanging on the nails.

"What's over there?" Barbara T. said, seeing Ruthie look that way.

"Nothing."

Barbara T. dropped her jump rope and ran into the lot. Ruthie took off after her. They were just movie stars' pictures but Ruthie didn't want Barbara T. to even know about them. Barbara T. was getting sand in her shoes. Barefoot, Ruthie overtook her.

Inside the billboards, Ruthie grabbed the pictures and stuffed them up under her sweater.

"Let's see," Barbara T. said.

"Tell me what O'Connor said."

"She didn't say anything. She just drew a line through Mitzi's name on the spelling chart. On all her charts. And Mitzi had one hundred in math, too. Now show me."

"You're lying. Mitzi stayed home because people like you kept making fun of her."

"Oh yeah?" said Barbara T. "Then how come Miss O'Connor gave someone else her seat?"

Ruthie stared. Barbara T. wouldn't think of making that up.

"Come on, Ruthie, you said you'd show me."

Slowly Ruthie pulled out the pictures.

Barbara T. grabbed the slick magazine photos, cooing over Mr. Dark Eyes, "Oh, isn't he handsome?"

"Where did they go?" Ruthie said almost to herself.

"To jail! Where do you think?" Barbara T. said. "They're gone for good and they're never coming back!"

"Stop lying, Barbara T.!"

"Don't you read the papers? It was on the front page: JAPS TO GO!"

"It's your fault!" Ruthie cried. "You and Shirl! Those boys! Calling her names! Breaking their windows!"

"They're traitors!" Barbara T. shouted, backing away.

"No—you! You're the traitors!" said Ruthie, gathering her shoes and socks. "All of you," she cried, sitting on the sidewalk, tying her laces.

As Ruthie started to run, the pictures slid down her sweater and onto the street.

"Where are you going?" Barbara T. shouted as Ruthie waited for the light at the corner.

Cars zoomed past. Ruthie buttoned her sweater to the neck against the rising wind.

As she crossed the street, she heard Barbara T. calling, "Ruthie Fox, you're going to get in trouble. You're not supposed to leave this block!"

Ruthie had to know. Crossing block after block, she was thinking, "They *will* be there—they have a store."

Finally the signs and stores of Japantown came into view. After the busy streets, these were strangely quiet.

The kite store was closed: No kites blew in the wind. The Nisei Grill was boarded up. The neon sign that blinked DAY-NIGHT was turned off.

Nearby, the Five-and-Dime, where the man sweeping in front had waved to Mitzi, was closed, too. A naked doll lay on its side in the window, its arms flung wide.

Ruthie ran to Joe's Groceries. A piece of cardboard was taped over the hole where the rock had traveled. If the cardboard was to keep people from stealing things, it wasn't necessary—the window was empty except for a handwritten sign:

146

Many thanks to our wonderful friends.
Hope to serve you again in the near future.
God be with you until we meet again.
Joseph Fujimoto
Mr. and Mrs. T. Fujimoto

A small American flag was propped alongside.

"Mitzi!" Ruthie shouted, knocking hard on the door. "Mitzi!"

Cupping her hands around her face, Ruthie pressed her nose to the glass. The shelves were empty. A few vegetables lay in open bins. A broom leaned against the entrance to the back stairs.

Ruthie knocked harder. "Mitzi," she called. "It's me!"

After waiting ten minutes and getting no answer, Ruthie walked the long way back through empty streets. The streetlights came on—her signal to go indoors—but all Ruthie could think about was the empty store.

She climbed the stairs to her house.

"Ruthie!" her father said when she entered the kitchen, "I just got in." He was holding a note and looked angry. "Your mother's out looking for you. Where've you been?"

They heard the front door.

"Hank!" her mother called, frightened. "I can't find her—"

"She's here, Maggie."

"Thank God!" her mother said, rushing in.

"Mommy, they're gone!"

"Ruthie, don't ever do that again. I told you to be in when the streetlights come on—"

"But Mitzi's gone. Everything: Joe's Groceries, the Nisei Grill . . ."

"Hank, do you hear that?" Ruthie's mother said.

Her father nodded solemnly.

"They gave them no time," her mother said, unbuttoning her coat. "We didn't think it would happen so fast." She sat down.

"Why didn't you tell me?" Ruthie said.

"Honey, we tried to the night of the blackout. You wouldn't listen."

"Where did they go?" Ruthie asked.

Suddenly stern, her mother said, "Ruthie, you shouldn't have gone all that way alone, without permission."

"She's not gone for good, is she? Barbara T. said they're never coming back."

"Oh, honey, of course, they're coming back."

"But where are they?"

Her mother looked at her father.

148

"Cookie, we don't really know," he said. "The government is relocating everyone in Japantown. Everyone with Japanese ancestry has to report. The army's in charge now."

"Can't I see her?"

He shook his head. "Maybe later."

"No one was there at all?" her mother asked.

Ruthie shook her head.

"It makes me sick," her mother said. "It just makes me sick."

"We could all use some food," her father said.

For the first time in her life, Ruthie had no appetite.

The next day after school Ruthie stood barefoot in the sand behind the billboards. Low white fog drifted past. All the treasures lay at her feet: the chain, the earring, the doll, the lipstick. She had two new pictures, which she hung on the crossbar.

Picking up the doll, she brushed sand from the kimono and silky hair. The hair ornaments and fan were broken. She placed the doll between the pictures.

Next she picked up the chain and the blue earring and rubbed them on her pants to make them shine and put them on either side of the doll.

149

The lipstick was the only thing left. Ruthie tore off a rectangle of cardboard from an old soap box and, lying on her stomach, opened the tube and wrote:

TREASURES OF THE DROWNED

She rested the sign against the back of the billboard below the doll's feet.

Stepping back, she looked it over.

It looked like a grave.

Ruthie remembered how Mitzi had stood up to Shirl in all the fights; how she wasn't afraid to shove Shirl back on April Fool's Day.

Ruthie kicked the sign over. She scratched out the name and buried the sign so the name would stay a secret, then put the treasures in an old carton she found.

"Mitzi's coming back," Ruthie said to herself, carrying the box home. "She's coming back and we're going skating and riding the rides at Playland, and we're going to shoot baskets and—even if we have to walk the whole way—we're going to the Tea Garden where we'll climb the Moon Bridge and make a wish. I don't care what Barbara T. says. I don't care what the paper says or the government says or the army says. She's coming back."

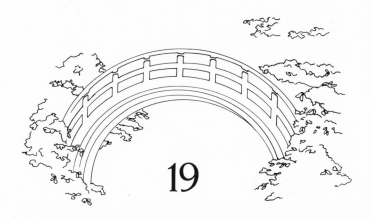

19

Necessity or Disgrace?

When Ruthie got home, she transferred the treasures to a clean box, along with Mitzi's blue mittens from Sutro's, and shoved it under her bed. She dug around in her desk for some stationery, found a sheet, then decided her desk was too crowded to write on. At the kitchen table, Ruthie wrote:

San Francisco, California
April 7, 1942

Dear Mitzi:
How are you?
I am fine.

151

I am sending this to your store. Daddy says the Post Office will find you.
I went to see you but nothing was there.
I miss you.
Where are you? What are you doing?
It's boring here. There's nothing to do.
In school our Victory Garden's leaves came up. Yours didn't yet.
Do you have a Victory Garden there?
Please write.

Love, your friend,
Ruthie

XXXXXX OOOOOO
PS. My address is on the outside.

The next day Ruthie raised her hand in class. "Miss Lewis," she said when she was called on. "Where did Mitzi from Miss O'Connor's class go?"

Some of her classmates sent Ruthie puzzled looks.

They don't even know she's gone, she thought.

"Ruthie, did you see the news this morning?" her teacher said.

Ruthie shook her head.

"Bataan has fallen. General MacArthur has surrendered to the Japanese. He has left the

Philippines. Our soldiers were taken prisoner."

Faces registered shock as hands went up with questions.

As awful as the war news was, Ruthie still wanted to know about Mitzi. She raised her hand.

When she was called on, she asked, "Miss Lewis, do you know where Mitzi went?"

"No," her teacher said, "but we are all safer with those people gone."

Ruthie stared. She wondered if she had heard right.

"Yes, Ruthie?" her teacher said in an exasperated tone when Ruthie's hand went up again.

"Miss Lewis, how can someone like Mitzi be dangerous?"

"I didn't say she was," Miss Lewis said, "but you wouldn't want her separated from her family, would you?"

Ruthie said, "Mitzi's father was in the First War and her brother's in this one!"

"I didn't call on you, Ruthie. Do you know how many men we've lost in the Philippines? Thousands. And thousands more are now prisoners. The Japs—who have done this—have only one loyalty: to Japan. No matter where they live."

Ruthie's face burned.

"And please try to control your temper! Raise your hand before you speak," her teacher added.

Suddenly Ruthie found herself hating the teacher she had loved all year.

She raised her hand again.

Miss Lewis ignored it and pulled down the wall map to show where Bataan was.

Bev turned around in her chair and sent Ruthie a look that said she was surprised, too, at Miss Lewis.

Suddenly their teacher said, "These people you're asking about, Ruthie, are lucky to be treated kindly, considering how the Japs are treating our men."

But all Ruthie could think of were the European refugees in the newsreels running from bombs, pushing their belongings up bumpy roads in wheelbarrows.

"If you don't know where they are," she blurted out angrily, "how do you know how they're treated?"

Miss Lewis' eye flashed. Someone gasped.

I've done it now, Ruthie thought.

"For that impertinence, you can stay after school, Ruth!" her teacher said.

Ruthie glared at Miss Lewis—the person she had thought was wonderful. Just last December she and Shirl had sat in the schoolyard shivering, more upset at the thought of Miss Lewis not coming back than at war being declared!

And I felt so sorry for her when her fiancé died, too, Ruthie thought angrily.

Shirl, across the aisle, was looking at their teacher with beaming eyes.

Ruthie looked around the room. If her classmates thought there was something wrong with locking Mitzi Fujimoto up, you'd never know it—everyone was so full of the news from Bataan.

When class broke for recess, Bev came up to Ruthie.

"I never thought she was like that," she said, looking back at their teacher.

"Me neither," Ruthie said.

"My mother said that they could take only one suitcase for each person," said Bev. "That's for everything they own! And one knife, fork, and spoon."

For the first time Ruthie really pictured what had happened. What would happen to their store? to their things? "One suitcase!" she said. "She wouldn't even be able to take her ice skates!"

"Ice skates take up a lot of room," Bev agreed.

"My mother says," said Ruthie, "that a lot of good farmland—some of the best in the state—

is going cheap now. The banks are snapping it up. People are getting rich on this, Bev."

And we worried so much, Ruthie thought, that someone would find out Mitzi lived outside the district. We thought that was the worst thing that could happen.

After school Ruthie had to write *I will not be rude to my teacher* a hundred times on the blackboard. Neither she nor Miss Lewis spoke.

The next afternoon, Ruthie sat in the music room with her class and Miss O'Connor's, her book on her lap, waiting restlessly for the elderly teacher to blow on her pitch pipe and start the first song.

Instead, Miss O'Connor looked sharply at them over her glasses.

What now? Ruthie thought. "Uh-oh" never put up with any fooling around.

"I've heard," Miss O'Connor said, "that some children from this school went into Japantown and broke store windows."

Her eyes searched the faces before her.

How did she know?? Ruthie wondered, then remembered that "Uh-oh" was a wizard. She could see behind her back.

Several children began whispering.

"Silence!" the teacher said. "I want you to know that if I find out who was responsible, that person or persons will not only answer to the principal, they will answer to *me* for such lawlessness and cowardly behavior!"

Ruthie whispered to Trevino next to her, "Too bad the boys who did it are in sixth and out of her reach."

Trevino gave Ruthie a surprised look. Ruthie had never told anyone about it before.

"As some of you know," Miss O'Connor continued, "a number of our friends and neighbors, many of them *citizens*"—hitting the last word hard—"have just been rounded up like criminals to be shipped to God-knows-where only because they or their forefathers happened to be born in the wrong country."

Ruthie's eyes widened. Yesterday the teacher she had loved told them that this was all fine. Today, the teacher she always disliked was saying just the opposite!

"One of those individuals," Miss O'Connor said, "was my student, Mitzi Fujimoto—Yes, Shirley?"

"But they were spying," Shirl said, pushing hair out of her eyes, "—sending secrets back to Japan."

"Oh?" Miss O'Connor said, her eyes lively. "You know this for a fact?"

"Everyone does."

"Everyone knows that thousands of people are disloyal?"

"I heard—"

"I asked for facts. Not what you've heard."

Shirl looked uncomfortable. "Well, no, Miss O'Connor, but—"

Ruthie wanted to grin.

"Unless you know what people think and feel," Miss O'Connor said, "by looking into their hearts like Superman—"

Several children giggled.

"—you don't really know, do you?" the teacher continued.

"But—" Shirl said.

"That's why we have courts and laws. To look at facts—not at 'what we've heard.' So isn't it possible," Miss O'Connor drove on, her blue eyes ablaze, "that we've taken innocent people and locked them up for no better reason than that we're afraid?"

"They're not locked up," Shirl said. "They're in camps."

"I see. So after they've had a nice rest they can leave?"

"I . . . don't know. . . ." Shirl said, looking

more uncomfortable than Ruthie had ever seen her.

"Then maybe you shouldn't talk. We are at war with Germany and Italy, are we not?" Miss O'Connor said.

Shirl pressed her lips tight together and stared back, her face red and angry.

"Well, are we not?" "Uh-oh" said, looking around the room. No one else seemed willing to tangle with her.

"Has everyone lost their tongue? Aren't we presently at war with both Germany and Italy?"

"Yes, we are!" Ruthie said, her voice coming out louder than she meant it.

"Ah, someone knows what's going on in the world," Miss O'Connor said with a faint smile. "Yes—for those of you who haven't yet heard the news, we are at war with Germany and Italy as well as with the land of the Rising Sun. And yet," she continued, "I don't notice anyone locking up Geraldine's family—"

Ruthie couldn't remember who "Geraldine" was until she felt Trevino next to her stiffen.

"—or Eric's, whose grandparents are from Germany—"

"Hey, I was born here!" little Eric Schultz said. "I'm American!"

"I didn't say you weren't, Eric," Miss O'Connor said. "Every single person in this room is descended from people who came from some other country. Unless there are some Cherokee or Mohicans present I don't know about."

"Uh-oh" waited, looking around. "Any Cherokee or Mohicans?"

The class broke into loud laughter.

Ruthie wanted to cheer. Finally, someone besides her parents was saying that Mitzi didn't deserve what happened to her.

"I don't suppose you're a Cherokee or Mohican, are you, Shirley?" Miss O'Connor said.

Shirl just shook her head.

Ruthie remembered too well Shirl's bullying and threats to Mitzi to feel sorry for her. Now *she's* got to take it alone, Ruthie thought. How do you like it, Shirl?

Ruthie saw Barbara T. joining in the laughter and she remembered how just yesterday they all cheered along with Miss Lewis. It's so easy to be part of the crowd, Ruthie thought, and never think for yourself.

Where *was* Mitzi? she wondered again.

"Nobody cares about Mitzi," Ruthie said under her breath, tired of the laughter.

"Hey, that's not true," Trevino said.

"Then why didn't you stand up for her,"

Ruthie whispered, "when everyone picked on her?"

"I didn't know her then," Trevino said. "I would now."

Sure, Ruthie thought, now that it's too late.

Later in the hall, Miss O'Connor called Ruthie over.

Uh-oh, Ruthie thought, I'm going to get it for talking in music.

"Have you heard from your friend Mitzi?" the teacher asked.

"No, Miss O'Connor," Ruthie said, surprised.

Miss O'Connor shook her head. "It's a disgrace what we've done, Ruth, a disgrace."

Ruthie nodded. She started to say something but tears came to her eyes. She couldn't speak. She wanted to throw her arms around the elderly teacher and sob. Instead they stood looking at each other.

Then, to Ruthie's shock, the teacher's face started moving—Miss O'Connor was smiling! She had very false-looking false teeth.

I wonder, Ruthie thought, if that's why she never smiles.

"When you do hear from Mitzi, dear," Miss O'Connor said, "tell her that we miss her."

Miss O'Connor missing someone?

Amazed, Ruthie smiled back. "I will," she said, wiping her eyes.

Boy! Mitzi's never going to believe this when I tell her! Ruthie told herself. Then she remembered.

When will that be?

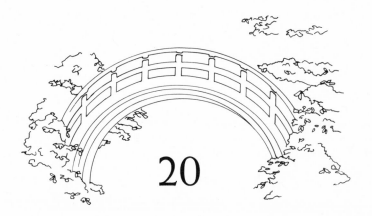

20

Letters from a Race Track

The following week Ruthie ate alone. She was waiting to hear from Mitzi and she didn't feel like talking to anyone, hearing them say how they would have stuck up for her if only this and if only that.

Standing in the schoolyard watching the other girls laughing with their friends and making plans for after school, Ruthie thought, It's as if she was never here at all. She wondered how she could wait for summer, two whole months away.

Just before Easter vacation, the Victory Garden came up. Each person in Miss Lewis' class received two radishes.

"They're good!" Bev said, taking a bite. "I always hated radishes."

"Me, too," Ruthie said, looking over to "Uh-oh's" class at the next plot watering their bean shoots. With one person missing.

In the sandlot after school Ruthie thought about Mitzi that first day during the drill when she stacked dominoes in a slinky row and made them dance.

Where was she? Back East? Chicago? Would they live in tents or cabins? With lots of trees? Would there be things to do?

Easter vacation came and went. When Ruthie returned to school, she ate with Bev and Trevino.

"Have you heard from Mitzi?" Bev asked.

Ruthie shook her head. "I don't even know where she is."

"She didn't even get to finish fifth grade," Trevino said. "But it was for their own protection. People were picking on them."

"Would you like to be locked up for your own protection?" Ruthie asked.

Trevino shrugged. "If my country started the war, I'd deserve it."

"Your country did," Ruthie said. Italy was on Germany's side, even if it didn't start the war and nobody was mad at them.

"Hey!" Trevino said. "I'm not Italian—my parents are—"

"When the war's over," Bev put in quickly, "the first thing I'm going to do is get me a big strawberry milk shake."

"Not me," Trevino said. "What I miss is butter—real butter."

Every day afer school Ruthie looked for a letter. Just when she began to wonder if Mitzi would ever write, a letter came—three weeks after Ruthie had mailed hers.

Tanforan Assembly Center
California, U.S.A.
April 24, 1942

Dear Ruthie:
Your letter took a long time to get here.
I am fine. How are you?
We are at Tanforan.
My mother won't let me talk about it.
So I can't say anything.
No, we don't have a Victory Garden.

It's too muddy. The food is awful.
Don't tell I said that.
Do you still hunt for treasures?
                        Love,
                        Mitzi
PS. The food is not that bad. My mother would
kill me for saying anything.

Ruthie looked for a second page but that was it. Tanforan? That was a racetrack! When she was little she heard her father saying he was going there and she cried to be taken, thinking the name sounded circus-like: Tan-for-an.

Mitzi couldn't be living there!

Ruthie read the letter again. What was she doing? How did she feel? Nothing but "the food was awful" and it was muddy.

"It *is* the old racetrack," Ruthie's mother said that evening when Ruthie asked her about it. "I read it in the papers."

"*How* can you live in a racetrack?" Ruthie said.

"Not very comfortably, I'm sure," her mother said.

In her bed that night, Ruthie thought how Mitzi was only an hour or so away. It was worse than if she were in Chicago.

For days, Ruthie played in front of her house, hitting a ball against the white stucco, wondering how she could get Mitzi to tell her more. One day just as Mrs. Rothstein poked her head out of her window saying, "Ruthie, please, the noise!" Ruthie had an idea.

She ran inside and wrote:

San Francisco, California
April 29, 1942

Dear Mitzi:
How are you? I am fine.
I'm sorry the food is awful.
You know what O'Connor did? Made a big speech in music saying it was a DISGRACE that you had to go away. And she stopped me in the hall! I thought to bawl me out for talking but she said THAT SHE MISSED YOU!!!
How about that???
You know why "Uh-oh" never smiles?
False teeth! Mitzi, you're just an hour from here. Do they let people visit? Listen, I have a plan. I know you're not supposed to but please tell me about it there. I am your best friend and I promise not to tell.
Not even my parents.

*This is how you can. No one will know. Use
this code:*

A B C D E F G H I J K L M N O P Q R S T U V W X Y Z

Z Y X W VU T S R Q P O N M L K J I HG F E D C B A

*When you want a letter from the top you use
the one right under it. Here is my message:*
DSVIV WL BLF HOVVK?
*Our radishes came up. I didn't used to like rad-
ishes but I do now.*
*School's going to be out in 5 weeks! I can't wait!
What's school like there?*

Love,
Ruthie

XX OOO
PS. No, I don't look for treasures anymore.

Two weeks after Ruthie mailed her letter,
she still had no reply. "Why doesn't she write?"
she said to her mother as she came up the
stairs.

"Please, Ruthie, I've got a headache," her
mother said. "It was mobbed at the store. Make
yourself a sandwich—I'm too tired to cook. And
don't talk."

Ruthie wished her father were home more often or that she could go away somewhere and live by herself.

She began to wonder if her code got Mitzi in trouble. Or if her mother found the letter. But Mitzi would sneak a letter out somehow.

Ruthie had even been thinking of helping Mitzi escape, like Huck and Tom did with Jim. But she knew that was crazy—a kid's game.

Finally a letter came! Ruthie ran to her room and shut the door. Some was in code! She read the easy part first:

Tanforan Assembly Center
May 15, 1942

Dear Ruthie:
Thank you for your letter. You're not supposed to tell the code when you use it! I shouldn't write this but I will. Don't tell your parents.

Oh good, Ruthie thought, reading on.

We live RM GSV HGZOOH *and it is always* XILDWVW *and* MLRHB. *We can hear the next* UZNROB GSILFTS *the* DZOO.
There isn't enough of ZMBGSRMT. *Some mothers*

169

WLM'G SZEV VMLFTS WRZKVIH *and some old people* WLM'G *have their* NVWRXRMV.

I miss my own YVW. *I wish we were at the* OLG, *too. Yes, now people can visit. It would be nice if you could.*

The DLIHG KZIG, *Ruthie, is that there are* UVMXVH ZOO ZILFMW FH *and the* TZGVH ZIV MVEVI LKVM.

RG'H ZDUFO SVIV.

Love,

Mitzi

XXXXX OOOOO

PS. Do you have a picture to give me?

She could visit! Excitedly, Ruthie began to work out the coded parts.

When she finished, she read it again. Something must be wrong.

The last two lines: "It's awful here," and . . . "fences all around us and the gates are never open."

Could it really be?

Sitting on her bed, Ruthie worked it out a second time. It came out the same.

She stared out the window at the strip of ocean.

So Barbara T. had been right, after all.

For days, Ruthie put off writing. Nothing she'd ever known was like this. When she visited what could she say? Mitzi must need so much. What should she bring? She didn't know the words to tell her it would be all right, to cheer her up, and there was no one to ask. If she told her parents what Mitzi had written, she might get her in trouble—and she'd promised she wouldn't.

Ruthie asked her father about visiting. He said, "If you can wait till the Sunday after next, can do!"

Ruthie rushed to write:

San Francisco, California
May 26, 1942

Dear Mitzi:
I feel so ZDUFO about what you GLOW NV.
But I have GOOD NEWS! I'm going to visit.
In just 2 Sundays. Not this one coming—my father has to work—but the next one!
Do you want some comic books? And cookies? I have a new recipe for butterscotch!
I play basketball with Trevino Saturdays.
She's OK but all she likes is sports.
School will be out in just TWO WEEKS!!
My mother wants me to go to Y Day Camp. I

171

don't want to. She might make me. Ho-hum.
Do you have classes? Like what?
I hate Giraffe Lewis now.
I can't wait to see you!

Love,
BLFI UIRVMW,
Ruthie Fox

PS. You can have this picture. It's not very
good. The sun was in my eyes and that dress
makes me look fat.

Ruthie put aside five comic books and a Nancy Drew mystery. The Sunday after school let out she'd be taking them to Mitzi.

On the last Friday of classes, Ruthie, Bev, and Trevino stood in the yard watching the sixth-grade boys and girls looking grown-up in their best clothes, walking two by two into the dance room for their graduation party.

"Look, there's the neighborhood paperboy!" Ruthie said.

"Pete Preovolous," Bev said, sighing.

Pete's short brown hair was slicked back. With his olive skin and black eyebrows and his white shirt and tie, he looked so handsome Ruthie couldn't help staring.

"Lucky you!" Trevino said.

Ruthie looked at Trevino with surprise. Trevino liked boys??

"I don't even know him," Ruthie admitted. "He delivers the *Call* and we take the *Chronicle*."

The three girls watched the line of sixth graders enter the dance room. Dressed up, the class a year ahead of them suddenly seemed much older and far away—as if they were already part of another world.

Watching Pete, Ruthie wished she wasn't afraid of boys. Then she could ask to ride his bike.

The Sunday came when Ruthie and her father were supposed to drive to Tanforan but no letter had arrived to set up the meeting.

"Maybe it got lost in the mail," Ruthie said. "Can't we go anyway?"

"I don't think so, Cookie," her father answered. "With gasoline rationed, we can't drive all that way on the off chance they'll let us in. Wait for her letter, and I promise I'll take you."

Ruthie's mother signed her up for the Y Day Camp, a long trolley ride away. Ruthie hated it. She didn't know anyone and stood around feeling stupid.

After several weeks, when Ruthie had given up hope of hearing, a letter came. Instead of Mitzi's familiar office stationery, it was her own coming back. The envelope was stamped UNDE-LIVERABLE. RETURN TO SENDER.

She opened it. Her picture fell out.

Mitzi never saw it.

So they'd gone again. But where?

Ruthie had to wait until July for an answer. The letter that came was torn and had been cancelled three different times. One stamp said *Nevada*.

Ruthie tore it open. It was dated two months earlier.

Tanforan
May 29, 1942

Dear Ruthie:
I just found out that we're leaving.
I don't have time to write.
I'm sorry you couldn't visit.
Everyone is rushing.
Someday we'll be back.

Love,
Your friend,
Mitzi Fujimoto

Leaving for where?

Ruthie put away the comic books and the Nancy Drew and stared at the gray strip of ocean out her bedroom window. Now she would never visit her.

That night when her mother was chopping cabbage for cole slaw, Ruthie said, "Where are they going now, do you think?"

"To another camp, I'm afraid, honey. Farther away," her mother said. "Tanforan was a temporary camp. They're being moved to a permanent one."

Ruthie stared at the chopping bowl.

"I wish I knew more, honey," her mother said, wiping her forehead with the back of her hand.

Gone. Really gone now.

In her room, Ruthie added the new letter to the box of treasures under her bed. Barbara T. was only partly right. She said Mitzi would never come back. But she would.

The next Saturday Ruthie put on her jacket and took the trolley to the beach. She climbed the long hill to the Cliff House and Sutro's. The wind was wild: It blew through Ruthie's clothes as she walked to the rail where she and Mitzi once screamed into the crashing waves. Looking down, Ruthie remembered their silly fight about whether ships were worth seeing or not and wished she could bring that time back.

She looked up. The sea lions on Seal Rocks seemed not to feel the cold: They dove and nuzzled each other and slapped their tails and honked at the sun.

If she couldn't be a person, Ruthie decided, she wanted to be a seal, playing all day long with its friends.

For a long while she stood there, staring into the gray water stretching far into the Pacific where the war was still raging—there, and here at home.

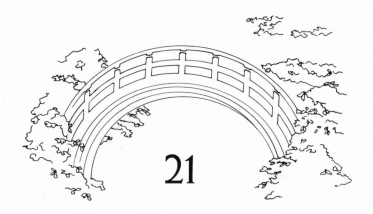

21

Lost: Two Braids;
Found: One Bike

Ruthie waited for a letter with Mitzi's new address but none came.

"Where do you think she is?" she asked her parents one night in July.

"There's nothing in the papers," her father said.

Her mother said, "I tried to call something called 'Wartime Civil Control' but they said they're overworked and understaffed. They couldn't help me."

"I read there're some camps in Nevada," her father said.

"And Utah and Arizona," her mother added.

All Ruthie could picture was desert and mountains. Nothing real to put Mitzi in.

Ruthie had waited so impatiently for summer. Now that it was here, the days dragged. She met a few kids at the Y camp but it wasn't like being a Starving Romanian or a member of a club. Ruthie found herself looking forward to fall when her class would be the oldest in the school.

Now it stayed light until nearly her bedtime. One hot evening Ruthie went outside to sit on her stairs and saw Pete the paperboy on foot collecting his money door-to-door.

"Hi," she said.

"You're in Lewis's class, aren't you?" he answered.

"Used to be," Ruthie said. "You graduated!"

Pete grinned, his teeth white against his dark skin.

Ruthie got up all the nerve she could muster and said, "Pete, could you show me how to ride your bike?"

He pretended to groan. "Catch me tomorrow," he said.

Ruthie wondered if that was a yes or no.

The next day she hurried back from camp to wait.

There he was! Gliding down the block, tossing the papers overhand with a smooth motion as he steered with his knees.

Ruthie couldn't imagine anything more wonderful than being able to ride like that.

"Hi!" she called out.

"Hi, Ruthie!"

He knew her name! "Pete, can I ride it?" she asked.

He pretended to turn and ride the other way.

"Pete, you promised!" she called, although he hadn't.

"OK, OK," he said, grinning as he pulled his bike over. "Just once down the block."

"I don't know how," Ruthie said, smiling.

"What??" Shaking his head, Pete took the heavy bag of papers off the back wheel and, pushing his sweater sleeves up, held the bike steady for her, pretending to be annoyed.

The seat looked higher than Ruthie had expected but she managed to get her leg over the high crossbar. She was thankful she was wearing shorts and not a dress. Pete walked her up and down the block while she pedaled.

That night she wrote Mitzi:

Guess what?!! I can ride a bike!
Remember the paperboy Pete? He's really nice!
And cute! He held on and then let go.
Before I knew it I was riding! I almost pretended
I couldn't so he'd still have to help. Ha. Ha.

Ruthie had nowhere to mail the letter so she put it in a cigar box on her desk.

Every day after camp she waited for Pete and every day he let her ride up and down the block.

Ruthie dreamed of having a bike of her own and riding everywhere but no one was making bikes with a war on.

One day as she waited for Pete, he came by with a girl.

She wore lipstick and Pete's jacket.

After he introduced them Ruthie said she'd hurt her knee and didn't feel like riding.

That night she wrote:

Mitz: Pete came by with this awful girl. I really
didn't like her. I know he just thinks of me as a
kid and I'm sure not in love with him or any-
thing but I really don't want to ride his bike

*with her there. What should I do?? I wish you
were here to tell me!*

The next day after camp, Ruthie stayed
inside. She saw Pete and the girl again and after
that she went inside when it was time for him to
be coming by.

One afternoon, Ruthie was hitting a ball
against the stucco face of her house, feeling mis-
erable, when Mrs. Rothstein looked out.

Mitz: Guess what?? Ruthie wrote.

She imagined Mitzi answering her.

Mitzi: You were elected President.
Ruthie: Seriously. *I got a bike!*
Mitzi: How?
Ruthie: From my landlady!
Mitzi: Is that a joke?
Ruthie: No! It was in the basement. An
   old one.
Mitzi: I thought she was too fat to ride.
Ruthie: She said it was there when they
   bought the house. She forgot
   about it until she saw me on
   Pete's.

Mitzi: Wasn't it old and rusty?

Ruthie: Sure, but I got the tires pumped up at the gas station. And I'm painting it. Isn't Mrs. Rothstein nice?

Mitzi: I bet she just wanted you to stop hitting the ball against the house!

Now Ruthie rode her bike through all the neighboring blocks. She learned to let go of the handlebars and balance with her knees. On Saturdays she rode all over the city. One day she traveled to Golden Gate Park. She visited the de Young Museum and the Aquarium, remembering teasing Mitzi about it being spooky the night she came for dinner.

The Japanese Tea Garden was next to the de Young. Ruthie wasn't sure if she wanted to go in.

The sign still said, CHINESE TEA GARDEN.

Under the tiled pagoda roof, the high gates were closed. Behind a wall of smooth unpainted wood the garden was hidden away.

Ruthie thought of the day, six months before, when she and Mitzi had said it was their favorite place in the whole world.

That night at dinner Ruthie said to her parents, "I'm afraid Mitzi isn't all right. I haven't gotten a letter since she left Tanforan."

"Wartime, Cookie," her father said. "Everything takes longer—the mail, trains, getting resettled." He bit into his bread. "Maybe she hasn't got a stamp!"

Ruthie looked at her mother, whose eyes said she didn't agree.

"Honey . . ." her mother said, "maybe Mitzi doesn't feel like writing."

"Why not?"

"Well, she's been through an awful lot."

"She could tell me about it," Ruthie argued. Hadn't Mitzi confided in her about Tanforan?

"Honey," her mother said, "when you're treated unfairly, sometimes you stop trusting people. Even your best friends."

"But Mitzi wouldn't blame me!" Ruthie said.

"I didn't say that," her mother answered. "I said she's been through a lot. She might only trust people who've been through it, too."

Ruthie stared at her mother. Mitzi not trust her? Ruthie felt ready to cry. It was so frustrating. If her mother was right, it meant that even if she saw Mitzi tomorrow, Mitzi might not want to see her.

"Oh, come on, you two," her father said. "I'll bet Mitzi just can't find a stamp!"

Fall came and Ruthie started the sixth grade. She wrote Mitzi:

School's boring. I eat lunch with Bev and Trevino. Bev says, "What do you think of our teacher . . ." and it's just some little thing that's different from Miss Lewis. Then Trevino says, "Dibs on being pitcher at kickball!" The boys run across the line between their yard and ours and throw water at us or call us "Pinhead." You should see Shirl and Barbara T. chase them back and giggle. Really dumb.

Ruthie remembered how much Mitzi hated Shirl and Barbara T. and crossed out the parts about them.

Hearing that the cafeteria needed helpers, Ruthie went down to volunteer. That night she wrote:

I have a job. In the cafeteria scraping plates! I get to leave class early. The halls are real quiet. I can pick out anything I want to eat—free! The little kids are so shy when they bring their trays up. My mom says, "Ruthie, we can feed you, you know," but I said the yard wasn't any fun anymore. What are you doing?

In the spring Ruthie went to the beauty parlor on Anza Street and had her braids cut off. It was strange to see a part of herself lying on the tile floor but she liked the light feeling her head had with the long hair gone.

I don't know if I look good in short hair or not, she wrote.

> *You could tell me if you were here. Is your hair different? Guess what? Trevino won't answer to anything but "Gerry" now. But we can't remember! When we say "Hey, Trevino" does she get mad! She cut off her braids, too. She looks real good! All of us have autograph books. I asked "Uh-oh" O'Connor to sign. She wrote: "To thine own self be true, And it must follow as the night the day, Thou canst not then be false to any man." Kind of gives you a chill, doesn't it? It's by Shakespeare. Bev wrote on the back page, "By hook or by crook, I'll be the last in this book." Trevino wrote: "When you're old and gray, remember we were friends this day."*

Ruthie added:

> *I wish you were here to sign my autograph book. I'm going to save it forever.*

She imagined Mitzi signing it and writing: *"To my best friend Ruthie. I miss you and will never forget you."*

June came and Ruthie's class, dressed in their best, walked to the dance room in pairs, a girl with a boy, watched by fifth graders as once she and Bev and Trevino—Gerry—had watched Pete Preovolous' class.

In a new peach-colored dress she prayed she wouldn't spill cake on, Ruthie looked around, her head feeling strangely light with short hair. She was surprised at how grown-up her classmates suddenly looked: Gerry in a blue dress with matching bows in her hair and white gloves, Bev all in white, turning around and smiling with tears in her eyes. Ruthie's partner, little Eric Schultz, was now taller than she was. The boys all wore ties with white shirts and dark pants and looked better than Ruthie ever imagined they could.

Seeing Bev wipe tears away, Ruthie realized she didn't feel sad. She had spent almost her whole life within the walls of John Sutter Elementary School—under the mural in the auditorium of John Sutter panning for gold. She was ready to go. Looking up at the sea gulls on the roof taking the sun, Ruthie thought she might miss them, swooping down for their noontime scraps—even though she always screamed and ducked for fear of getting hit by droppings.

Mitzi, are you dressed up somewhere, holding an autograph book? Ruthie wondered, as she looked at Mitzi's old classmates behind her in line. There was no answer: only the forward progression of sixth graders entering the decorated dance hall for their last party at Sutter School.

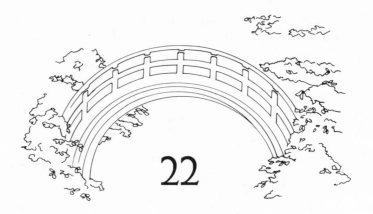

22

The Night the Bells Rang

The unmailed letters to Mitzi now filled a cigar box. When Ruthie looked at them and thought how it had been over a year since Mitzi had written, sometimes she couldn't help feeling angry. But sometimes it seemed much longer than a year because so much had changed. Still, if she were in Mitzi's place, no matter what—depressed, ashamed of what she'd been through, bitter—Ruthie felt sure she would write. If only to say she was OK.

Because Mitzi hadn't, it hurt. Ruthie now

wrote only when she had no one else to talk to. Like when she started junior high:

Boy! Is this place enormous! So many faces I don't know! We have lockers and only 5 min. to get to them between classes! Some days all I do is RUN! We have P.E.—that's gym—and social studies and we get to pick our own teachers. Oh, the other day I was going down the hall feeling kinda lost when I heard "Ruthie!" You know who it was? Pete! the paperboy! He was really friendly. Some 8th graders, you know, won't even talk to us. I really had a crush on him. I never told you, but I did.

Sometimes at a football game, or standing at her locker joking with a classmate, Ruthie would think guiltily: Mitzi's missing all this. But it happened less and less often as Ruthie would get caught up in the busyness of school life and forget.

The following spring she wrote:

Mitz: We finished the 7th grade. You wouldn't recognize anybody. Gerry Trevino is super-feminine now and never gets near a playing field.

189

*She's real pretty and—would you believe—
giggles! Bev's in orchestra—I never see her.
Shirl went back to Iowa with her family to wait
for her dad to come home. And Old Toothpick
Legs has filled out! She lost her freckles and
hangs all over some boy from 10th grade. I
never see any of them anymore. Do you look the
same? More later.*

But Ruthie didn't write more. Not for a long
time. Too much was happening. Italy surrendered
and everyone was saying that the war would soon
be over. Magazines were full of articles about pre-
paring the country for the returning servicemen.
When planes flew overhead, Ruthie didn't even
glance up.

September came and with it, the eighth
grade. Ruthie signed up for dramatics and Spanish
and made new friends. At night she pinned up
her hair and polished her shoes and couldn't wait
for school the next day.

One night the following spring Ruthie was
sitting on her bed reading the paper when a photograph caught her eye. It was of the returning
Nisei units. They had taken "huge losses," the
article said, and "fought with exceptional
bravery."

All this time, Ruthie thought, while I finished fifth and sixth grades and am halfway through junior high—they've been fighting. Mitzi's brother and his friends. Ruthie scanned the faces of men with missing legs and arms but it was too hard to remember a face from a photo on Mitzi's bureau three years before. She ran down the list of those missing in action. Sab wasn't there. Ruthie prayed he was all right. After all the Fujimotos had been through, if Sab didn't come back—that would be too much.

Mitzi, where are you? Ruthie wondered again. What's happened to you?

During Easter vacation Ruthie decided to give a pajama party and invite her new friends. Someone had given one the month before and it had been fun—staying up all night talking and telling jokes.

All that day Ruthie cleaned, discouraged at how long it took to straighten drawers, neaten her closet, vacuum her rug. When she was in the kitchen putting a batch of cookies in the oven and checking the soft drinks and chips, her mother called from the living room, "Honey, did you clean under your bed?"

"Yes!" Ruthie said. She hadn't, though. Would anyone look?

If they did and found something silly, they'd tease her no end.

Lying on her stomach, Ruthie groaned at the clutter. A library book months overdue, a textbook she'd lost, a missing shoe, socks with no mates and . . . the old box of treasures.

She had completely forgotten it. Sitting up, she pulled it onto her lap.

Carefully, Ruthie opened the lid, remembering the magic the box had once held.

The old movie stars' pictures were faded. How could she and Mitzi have liked those old glamour boys so much? Oh, the doll! Gently she lifted the delicate porcelain figure, its silk robes now faded. The doll that had caused so much trouble. The paper fan was broken and so were the tiny hair ornaments, but that had happened long ago. The treasures—the little chain, the tarnished earring, the lipstick—looked just the same but far more battered than she'd remembered.

How much mystery ten-year-old Mitzi and Ruthie had imparted to these ordinary objects! Ruthie smiled to herself. She had to admit a part of that mystery remained as she pulled off the lipstick top and turned the battered base. Again the purply-red stick rose up. Ruthie almost started to write T.D. on her arm.

Oh, Ruthie, she told herself, what are you keeping it for? Mitzi will never come back. And even if she does—what would she want with this junk?

It's not junk, said a voice in Ruthie's head. *It was our magic.*

Closing the tube, Ruthie returned it and the other treasures to the box. As she put it high up on her closet shelf, she noticed a strange smell. Was something burning?

Germany surrendered in May. The papers and newsreels were full of American servicemen rolling their tanks into Europe, cheered by weeping thousands. All that was left now was Japan. Everyone believed the end would soon come.

One warm August night Ruthie and her parents were in their living room when they heard church bells pealing—first one, then another, then whistles and shouting. They ran to the window.

Everyone on the block was in the street.

The war was over.

That night Ruthie lay in bed too excited to sleep. Listening to the bells still pealing, she wanted to write down all her feelings. Turning on the light, she dug under the mattress for her diary.

Suddenly she sat up. Mitzi!

She'd forgotten all about her!

How could she?

It had been so long now. Ruthie counted up: three years and four months.

Did she know?

She must!

Ruthie grabbed a piece of paper.

V-J Day, August 15, 1945, she wrote.

MITZI! We were in the living room, Mom, Dad, and me when outside there was this shouting and bells. We looked out and EVERYONE on our block was there. Lots of people I've never seen before and Babs—that's what Barbara T. calls herself these days—and her folks and even old Mr. Rothstein! He danced around and hugged my mother and kissed me and forgot about his heart! I hugged and kissed Mrs. R. (that's what I call her now) and tears ran down her cheeks. She lost her sister to the Nazis. Mitz, I tell you, I was hugging and kissing people I never SAW before. EVEN Babs! I couldn't help it, I was so happy! And she was screaming and crying and kissing me, too. Someone had a saxophone and played "Happy Days Are Here Again," and we all danced and cried some more and then laughed and then cried again. Dad

*picked my mom up and swung her around. Oh
Mitz, I'll never ever forget it as long as I live!*

For a long while Ruthie lay in bed, listening
to the far-off church bells, thinking, It's over, it's
over.

How would Mitzi have celebrated? Not
with the dancing and kissing of strangers.

Ruthie saw Mitzi and her family and Uncle
Joe—maybe even with her brother—standing in
some cold flat desert under a black sky full of
stars, looking up.

The soldiers would put down their rifles and
say, "You're free."

Three years and four months.

If only she'd been here! Tears came to her
eyes as Ruthie imagined herself and Mitzi jumping around and laughing and kissing and crying
and just too happy to talk.

Will they come back? Ruthie wondered. I
hope, I hope, she wished as she dropped off to
sleep.

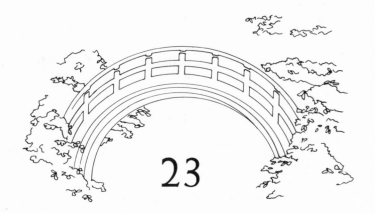

23

An Answer Arrives

Two weeks later Ruthie was coming back from the record store. She'd gotten a phonograph for her birthday and spent all afternoon sitting in a booth listening to records before deciding which one to buy. The new record was under her arm when she checked the mailbox at the bottom of the stairs.

She almost dropped it.

There was a letter from Mitzi.

Ruthie tore it open as she ran upstairs.

August 24, 1945

Dear Ruthie:
Do you remember me? We used to play together
on your block in the sandlot.

Did she remember? How could she *ask?*
The letter went on:

How are you? I am fine.
Isn't it wonderful that the war is over?
My favorite subjects are math and English.
What are yours?

Dramatics, Spanish, and lunch, Ruthie said
to herself.

You must think I'm terrible for not writing for
so long.

No, Ruthie thought. But why?

I can't really explain it, but I wanted to tell you
that we are coming back!

She *was!*

Uncle Joe has gone to San Francisco to look for
a store for us. (He says hello.) Do you still hunt
for treasures? And skate at Sutro's?

197

Ruthie's heart beat fast as she kept reading.

Maybe we could meet somewhere if you want to.
I'll let you know when I'll be back.
I hope you and your family are fine.
You can write me here:

Mitzi gave an address that wasn't a street but a route with a number and then *Jerome, Arkansas*.

Arkansas! What was she doing there?
The letter ended:

> Yours truly,
> Mitzi Fujimoto

"Yours truly"??

Ruthie stared at the words. That was what you put on an absence excuse for your mother to sign.

And "Fujimoto"? How many "Mitzis" did she think Ruthie knew?

Was Mitzi really as stiff now as the letter? Ruthie told herself maybe she was just uncertain, as she walked around the apartment with the words, SHE'S COMING BACK! going round and round in her head.

Arkansas! So far away! Not even in a city but a "route." Wasn't that like a farm?

Ruthie read the letter again and called her mother at work. Her mother was a buyer now and had her own phone.

"She's coming back!" Ruthie said when her mother answered.

"Mitzi?" her mother said. "You heard from her?"

"Yes! She wants to meet me!"

"Oh, honey, that's wonderful!" her mother said. "Then she's all right!"

When she hung up, Ruthie sat down and wrote:

August 29, 1945

Dear Mitzi:
Of course I remember you!!
It's FANTASTIC that you're coming back!!!
So GREAT!! I thought of you a lot and especially on V-J Day. I wish you could have been here. Listen, tell Uncle Joe to look for an apartment in the Anza Jr. High District. That's where I go and Mitzi, you'd really like it. There

are some great kids and I can introduce you. We have pretty good dances and our basketball team won the championship! Say . . . just one more year and we'll be in high school. You have to go to Washington. It's definitely the best in the city. Don't go to Lowell! They're our rivals! Hey, we're actually going to be starting our freshman year. Wow! We're getting old! No, I haven't ice-skated since we went to Sutro's. And you must be kidding about looking for treasures!

Ruthie didn't know what else to say. After pouring out her heart to Mitzi on paper all these years, suddenly she felt shy confronting the real person.

She added a PS:

Listen, give my best to your folks and Uncle Joe. My mom and dad are just fine, thanks.

Ruthie wanted to say something about Mitzi's hardships but was afraid of bringing it up. Kids hated you to talk about anything like that. Ruthie once visited a girl whose mother drank. You had to pretend not to notice.

Ruthie read her letter over and decided she

couldn't be like Giraffe Lewis and act as if Mitzi had just moved away.

She added a PPS:

> *Mitzi, I know you've been through a lot.*
> *BUT THAT'S ALL OVER NOW!*

How to sign?

Yours truly seemed ridiculous.

Love was too gushy.

Sincerely, your friend, Ruthie?

Was she still Mitzi's friend?

She really didn't know. Mitzi was so formal. Ruthie decided on *Sincerely, Ruthie.*

As she was sealing the envelope, Ruthie realized something. *What a dope!* She'd forgotten to say, yes, she would meet her!

She ripped open the envelope and added a PPPS:

> *Yes, I can meet you. When???*

She found a stamp and mailed the letter that afternoon.

In less than two weeks the answer came:

201

Sept. 6, 1945

Dear Ruthie:

Thanks for your letter!

There isn't time to write anything because we're leaving! I don't know our phone yet and if you write now the mail might come here. So can you meet me in Golden Gate Park in the Tea Garden? Under the Moon Bridge? How's September 25, Saturday, at one o'clock? If you can't, I'll understand.

Sincerely,
Mitzi

It was now the tenth. Two weeks!

Ruthie was so excited she couldn't think. She ran to the calendar and marked the date. Then she stared out the window at the strip of ocean.

Suddenly she was scared. What do you say to someone who's been locked up for three years? Who had everything taken away?

But Mitzi remembered the Moon Bridge. Maybe she wouldn't be so different, after all.

Ruthie saw herself and ten-year-old Mitzi walking to class, saying how the Moon Bridge was their favorite place: cattails and dragonflies, the great Buddha and giant goldfish, tea outdoors in little cups and climbing the high Moon Bridge and making a wish.

The Tea Garden.

She'd never gone back.

Why?

Was she waiting for Mitzi?

Afraid it would be too painful without her?

Or afraid that the garden wouldn't live up to her memories?

Ruthie didn't know.

She looked at the calendar space for Saturday, September 25, where she'd drawn a big red star.

She would find out.

At last!

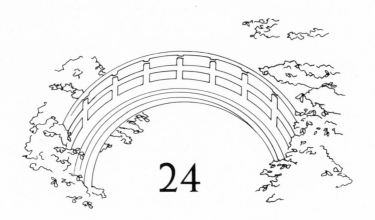

24

The Moon Bridge

Grabbing her jacket and purse, Ruthie hurried into the living room.

"How do I look?" she said to her mother. It was the Saturday Ruthie was meeting Mitzi.

"You look fine, honey," her mother said, glancing up from a book. She now had Saturdays off. "But won't you be hot? It's gorgeous out!"

Ruthie hadn't noticed the weather. She wanted to wear her new fall skirt and sweater. "No," she said, pulling the sweater away from her new bra that she was afraid made her look too big. "Mom," she said, "what if we don't recognize each other?"

"You will. Maybe not at first, but you will. Relax, honey," her mother said. "Tell Mitzi hello for me."

Ruthie nodded. "*If* she comes," she said.

"If she can, she will," Ruthie's mother said as Ruthie bent down for a kiss. " 'Hello' is so . . . puny . . . for what I want to say."

"I'll give her a BIG hello," Ruthie joked, making her eyes wide as she turned to leave. She added, "I wish my stomach would stop jumping around."

"Honey, you don't need a jacket!" her mother said, laughing.

Ruthie looked out the window at the blue sky. She liked having something to hold but she dropped the jacket on the sofa. Her purse would have to do.

" 'Bye!" she called from the hall.

What if I put my foot in it and say the wrong thing? she worried as she went down the stairs. How do you talk to someone who's been locked up three years?

As Ruthie shut the door, she looked up. Her mother was right: It was a gorgeous day. Blue skies and a slight breeze. Indian summer.

It's going to be all right, Ruthie told herself

as she waited for the bus. It's going to be all right.

A half hour later Ruthie stood in front of the Tea Garden, reading the sign, CHINESE TEA GARDEN. Ruthie sighed. Still.

Smooth walls of pale cypress hid the garden but the high gates under the tiled pagoda roof were flung open.

She was finally going in. Please let it be all right, Ruthie silently wished as she climbed the steps and passed under the gate.

The low rough fence of logs and bamboo that followed the twisting path bordering stone lanterns and flowering rhododendrons was as familiar to Ruthie as if she had seen it yesterday. So were the giant ferns and sunlit temples on the hill.

She drew a happy breath.

Nothing had changed.

A few feet away, cattails bowed in the breeze. Ruthie's stomach started to tighten as she crossed the stone footbridge. She could feel the shadow of the Moon Bridge above her.

No one waited at the bridge's base.

You're early, she told herself, checking her watch. Relax.

She looked up. Like a moon rising from the

sea, the smooth half circle of pale wood rose from rocks and shrubbery to arch high over her head. The bridge could be seen from all over the hilly garden. The same unpainted wood—like a giant carving—formed the curved rail and thin slats that served as steps. Ruthie smiled, watching children make the slow ascent, waving and calling to friends below. She remembered the fun of holding tight, stretching to reach from one slat to the next.

She looked toward the gate. No one like Mitzi was entering.

Stop worrying, she told herself. Aren't I here? She turned back to the bridge.

A weeping willow brushed the pond with its pale leaves. Dragonflies danced in clear sunlight on floating lily pads. The giant red goldfish she remembered so well flicked their tails past gleaming pennies on the pond's floor.

She sighed. She could stay here forever. But where was Mitzi?

Ruthie looked again at the passing faces. None were familiar.

Her eyes returned to the garden. So much was hidden from where she stood. To discover its secrets, you had to walk the crooked paths that disappeared into the trees and come out again by the Tea House. Otherwise you missed the carved tablets and pagodas and waterfalls she barely remembered.

Across the way was the Tea House. Ruthie could see hanging wisteria and the corner of a peaked roof. She remembered the tables and benches by the stream where you sat with your cup of tea and almond cookies, served by ladies in kimonos.

She and Mitzi would be sitting there—in just a little while! Laughing and trading reminiscences!

Mitzi?! Ruthie caught sight of an Asian girl's shiny dark hair. The girl turned her way. It was someone else.

What if this all turns out awful? Ruthie suddenly thought. What if she hates me for all I had while she was locked up?

Ruthie's stomach tightened. And will she want to talk about it? Suddenly Ruthie's skirt and sweater felt itchy and hot. Why did she have to wear them?

Maybe Mitzi won't come. Then I could enjoy the park and go home and not have to worry about saying the wrong thing or being guilty for not having suffered.

I could leave and she'd never know. I could just call and say I couldn't make it. Couldn't I?

No.

As Ruthie waited nervously, she watched the park's other visitors. French sailors in their red pom-pom berets passed Chinese soldiers in mandarin collars; American servicemen and women in khaki and navy blue; English sailors with HRH on their caps joking in accents Ruthie could hardly understand.

The whole world was gathered in the garden. Mitzi, Ruthie thought, the faraway lands of our Drowned Lady have come to us!

She checked her watch again: ten after.

When she turned to look back at the gate, she thought . . . could that girl . . . ? Ruthie raised a hand . . . hesitated . . . dropped it. She wasn't sure.

Dressed like an out-of-towner in a sleeveless dress, patent leather shoes, a purse and white gloves, the Asian girl carefully crossed the stone footbridge.

Ruthie's heart was beating fast. "Mitzi?" she said.

The girl looked up. Ruthie still wasn't sure.

"Ruthie?" the girl said.

It was! Ruthie's heart jumped. She stared trying to see the face she knew in this teenager.

"Mitzi!?"

"I thought it was you!" Mitzi said, in a new

209

Southern accent. "Ruthie, I'm sorry I'm late. I forgot how long the trolley took."

She was tall, as tall as Ruthie. Her bangs were now curled instead of straight and her hair reached her shoulders. Ruthie wasn't sure she would have recognized her in a crowd.

"That's OK, Mitzi!" Ruthie said, glad just to be looking at her, all desire to leave gone.

Mitzi smiled a hesitant smile—not the big one of before.

She's been so far away, Ruthie thought.

They looked up at the Moon Bridge. "It hasn't changed, has it?" Mitzi said.

"No, but you have!" Ruthie answered.

"You too, Ruthie," Mitzi said. "You look wonderful, Ruthie."

"So do you! You really do!" Ruthie said, unable to get used to the Southern lilt in Mitzi's speech.

Mitzi shook her head. "Oh, I don't know," she said. "My mother is so old-fashioned. She made me wear gloves."

"Oh," Ruthie said, "mothers are supposed to worry. Mine did when I got my bike. She says hello, by the way."

"Tell her hello back! You have a bike, Ruthie?"

"Mitzi, don't you remember?" Ruthie said. "I

wrote you all about it: how Pete the paperboy taught me, then Mrs. Rothstein—"

Mitzi slowly shook her head.

"Oh!" Ruthie said, feeling ridiculous. "Mitzi, I'm being so dumb! You see, I wrote you all the time—about everything. But I didn't have your address, so I never mailed anything!"

Pete Preovolous and the bike, Trevino changing from an athlete to a flirt, how lonely junior high was at first, the joy of V-J Day—all in a cigar box on a shelf in her room.

"I bet it was interesting," Mitzi said, politely.

What's the matter with me? Ruthie thought. I'm doing it again—talking about the first thing that comes into my head!

"Mitzi," Ruthie said, "how've you been? How's your family?"

"They're fine, thanks," Mitzi said. "And yours, Ruthie?"

"They're fine, too. Did I say my mother sends a big hello?"

They smiled at each other.

"You have a nice mother, Ruthie."

"Thanks. I'm surprised you remember. You only met her that once."

Mitzi stared. "Ruthie," she said, "my memories are the only things they let me keep."

For a moment, Ruthie felt so awful she couldn't say anything. Finally she said, "Mitzi, I felt so terrible . . . when you left."

"I know, Ruthie," Mitzi said.

They smiled at each other some more.

"Let's go to the Tea House," Ruthie said, "where we can sit."

The Tea House wasn't open for business yet but a lady in a tight Chinese dress with a high collar said they could sit on the bench.

It was chilly in the shadows under the peaked roof. Mitzi hugged her bare arms. Ruthie wondered if she, too, was thinking about the missing kimonos.

"I couldn't believe you were in Arkansas!" Ruthie said.

Mitzi nodded. "It was real hot," she said. "Like Sacramento. Except when it was cold. I've never been so cold in my life."

Arkansas. The little puzzle piece shaped like a coffee cup. It seemed as far away as Mars.

This meeting wasn't going anything like Ruthie had hoped. She thought they'd throw their arms around each other and tell each other everything.

"Are they really OK, Mitzi?" she asked. "Your parents? You?"

Mitzi nodded. She looked into Ruthie's eyes

and now Ruthie recognized her fully for the first time.

"We just got back a week ago, you know," Mitzi said. "We're doing OK. For my mom it was the first rest she'd had in years! But . . . well . . . Daddy. He never really got over it. It hurt him so much."

"I'm sorry," Ruthie said, wishing she could think of something better to say. "Mitzi, I wanted to visit you. You know, I had everything ready— comic books, cookies . . ."

"I know, Ruthie. I wish you could have."

They sat for a moment looking at each other.

Mitzi said, "It's hard to get used to you being grown-up!"

"You, too," Ruthie said. She paused. "Your father . . . what does he say . . . about what happened?"

Mitzi shrugged her one-shoulder shrug and looked at the bare table.

"He won't talk about it," she said.

"Not even to you?"

Mitzi shook her head. "Not to anybody." She looked up. "But Ruthie, how've you been? What are you doing these days?"

"Oh, I signed up for dramatics again and in P.E. we have to learn to swim—" Ruthie stopped.

She didn't want to talk about her easy life. "It's just so good to see you, Mitzi," she said. "Will you be going to Anza? It's a really good school."

"I'm not sure," Mitzi said quietly. "It depends on where we find a place."

"I thought you had."

"No, we're staying with friends."

"Oh," Ruthie said.

"But Anza sounds nice from your letter," Mitzi said.

Ruthie smiled and said, "You know, after you left Tanforan, I thought you were somewhere in the mountains. On V-J Day, I pictured you standing on a desert looking up at the stars and a soldier saying, 'You can go now, you're free.' "

Mitzi smiled. "We were free to leave way back in January, Ruthie."

"You *were*? Why didn't you?"

"My father wouldn't. 'Not till the war is over,' he said. 'Not until they *make* us leave.' I argued with him. I missed so much school—I wanted to start again."

"You didn't go to school?!"

"Oh, a medical student and college girl— they had to leave school—tried to teach us older kids, but without books . . ."

Ruthie thought of her school, not just the six courses a day—studying Spanish, memorizing scenes from *Romeo and Juliet*—but the life—jokes only friends understood, parties, talking about them the next day, football games, cheering for your team. . . .

"But you wrote that English and math were your favorite subjects," Ruthie said. She just assumed that Mitzi was in school—some kind of school—somewhere.

"The medical student taught me some algebra and a lady who had a book of Shakespeare read us parts," Mitzi said.

"Oh, Mitzi!" Ruthie said, appalled.

Looking at her old friend, she thought—I never really imagined her life at all.

"I hope I can catch up," Mitzi said, looking worried.

"Oh, I'm sure you can," Ruthie said, but feeling uncertain. "Lots of kids never study and still pass." But three years was a long time.

Wanting so much to take away Mitzi's worried look, Ruthie said, "Hey, a smart kid like you will be ahead of them in no time. Remember how 'Uh-oh' said she missed you?"

Mitzi smiled uncertainly. "Thanks for telling me that, Ruthie," she said.

"It's great you're back, Mitzi!" Ruthie said. "I wasn't sure you would . . ."

"A lot of people aren't coming back," Mitzi

said. "They remember too well . . . the way we were treated."

Ruthie nodded. "Then why . . . ?"

"My Uncle Joe. He has friends here—the lady whose address we used when I started Sutter? And other people who saved some of our things for us."

"Then there *were* some people who helped," Ruthie said, with relief. It was the first she'd heard about it. Even though she hadn't helped— she couldn't, of course—it made her feel less guilty.

"I heard stories in the camps about people taking care of houses and cars till neighbors got out."

"That's really good to know," Ruthie said. Suddenly she couldn't hold back. "Mitzi, I kept waiting to hear from you."

Mitzi looked at the nearby stream. Two black turtles were climbing onto a rock in the sun.

I shouldn't have said anything, Ruthie thought. "I mean," she explained, "I was worried. About how you were."

"I tried to write," Mitzi said.

Ruthie felt better. At least she wanted to.

"I tried to write," Mitzi repeated. "I even

started some letters but didn't mail them. After we left Tanforan, I thought . . . we're going to a regular house. Or something better. But instead it was just another camp. In Arkansas!" Mitzi said, shaking her head. "Remember when I first moved from Sacramento and said I missed hearing the rooster crow?"

"Well," Mitzi said, "I sure heard the rooster crow again."

They sat and watched the black turtles stretch their necks to the sun.

"Let's walk," Ruthie said. "It's freezing here in the shade."

The girls strolled up the path behind the Tea House. In a patch of sunlight, they stopped to admire a wooden shrine by a waterfall.

Do we have anything in common? Ruthie wondered. In some ways, she seems much older because she's suffered. In others, younger, because she's missed so much.

Breathing in the sharp smell of pine, Ruthie thought, can she have fun anymore? I can't imagine a friend who didn't joke.

Maybe she'll change, she thought. She's just gotten back.

"When you signed your letter 'yours truly,' "

Ruthie said, "you sounded a million miles away."

Mitzi stared at the path that was getting dust on her patent leather shoes.

"I just thought . . . you, here in San Francisco, with your friends and everything—might have forgotten me, Ruthie."

"Forgotten you?" Ruthie said, stopping in amazement on the path. But how could Mitzi know that Ruthie had never met anyone in the years after that she'd felt the same about? that for years she'd written to her even though Mitzi would never receive the letters?

"I still have the treasures," Ruthie said.

"You do?" Mitzi was surprised.

"In a box in my closet."

"We were so silly," Mitzi said.

"*What??*" Ruthie said. "We were not!"

Mitzi shrugged the one-shoulder shrug.

Ruthie was suddenly angry. "What does that mean?" she said.

"What does *what* mean?" Now Mitzi was angry.

"Saying we were 'silly,' " Ruthie said, "as if none of that matters now."

"I didn't say that!" Mitzi said, her eyes flashing.

"Well, what do you mean?" Ruthie repeated.

Some people behind them excused themselves and squeezed past them.

"We didn't know anything about the world, that's what it means," Mitzi said, when the people had gone. "We talked about silly things like the 'Drowned Lady's True Love,' how he'd 'never forget her.'"

"It was you who wanted him to never marry," Ruthie said. "I said of course he would. But what's wrong with saying he'd never forget her?"

"Some people forget real easily, Ruthie."

Ruthie looked at the ground. In the last two years, ever since she started junior high, she'd hardly ever thought of Mitzi.

"I tried to write you," she said. "I *did* write. *You* didn't write me back. You didn't trust me."

"That's not true!" Mitzi said.

Ruthie said nothing. They started walking. They passed ancient stone lanterns jutting into the pines.

Mitzi said quietly, "I didn't write anybody, Ruthie. You know if I had—it would have been you."

"No, I don't know that," Ruthie said, feeling her hurt well up at all the years of silence. "How would I know?"

"Ruthie," Mitzi said, "I thought about the things we did all the time! Almost Cocoa. You sliding around on those ice skates. Climbing the billboards to the very top."

Ruthie laughed. "Wasn't Almost Cocoa awful?" she said.

"Well . . . it wasn't *awful*," Mitzi said, smiling.

"Well, it sure wasn't cocoa!"

They both laughed. Ruthie said, "Mitzi—if you remembered those things—why didn't you trust me? Why didn't you let me help?"

"I don't know if I can put it in words," Mitzi said. "Ruthie—at Tanforan they came up to the fence and stared at us like we were in a zoo."

"Who did??"

"People. Kids. 'Good Americans.' "

"Oh, Mitzi." Ruthie felt sick. "How did you stand it?"

"Japanese are taught not to complain," Mitzi said.

"But when you're treated like that?" Ruthie said. "That's horrible!"

"And the people in the camps," Mitzi said, "acted as if nothing was happening."

"You're kidding," Ruthie said.

"They said, 'If our country wants us here,

it has its reasons.' They went about organizing things, working in the kitchen, helping get supplies and such. Others—like my dad and Uncle Joe—knew it was a terrible insult, but a Japanese would rather die than admit that. My father was so angry he couldn't talk about it."

"You said you couldn't, either."

Mitzi nodded.

Ruthie shook her head. "I wish I could have visited you," she said.

"You know they wouldn't have let you in, don't you?"

"What?"

Mitzi nodded. "When people visited, they had to talk through the fence. They handed packages over the barbed wire."

"Oh, Mitzi!" Unable to find words, Ruthie stared.

"It wasn't all awful," Mitzi said. "There were dances and baseball. But I couldn't talk to those kids, Ruthie. They acted like everything was fine. It was so unreal. All those smiling faces. I just kept to myself."

"That's how I felt after you left," Ruthie said.

Both of us, Ruthie thought, surrounded by people saying everything was fine. Both of us alone. But for me, that was only for a while, then I forgot. For Mitzi, it hasn't ended yet.

"Now do you see why I didn't write?" Mitzi said. "I hated everyone and everything."

"Including me?"

"Oh, no, Ruthie. I wrote letters to you in my head all the time."

They came out of the trees, into the sunlight, and stood in front of the great Buddha. The huge bronze statue sat cross-legged on a lotus blossom, its hand raised in peace. Ruthie thought again of V-J day. The crying and kissing.

She tried to understand what it would be like to stop talking. She thought, the Mitzi I remember was funny and bright and said what she thought and was adventurous and full of energy to try new things. Is she gone forever?

"Well, I'm glad you did write, finally," Ruthie said.

"I wanted to see you again," Mitzi said. "Oh!" she said and for the first time her face brightened with the big smile that Ruthie remembered. "Sab's back!"

"And he's OK?" Ruthie said as they headed down the hill.

Mitzi nodded proudly. "He's fine. He has a chestful of medals."

"That's great, Mitzi. I was jealous of you having a 'military secret,' remember? I thought it meant you knew the secret!"

Mitzi smiled as they walked down to the Moon Bridge.

Two little girls were at the pond's edge, peering past the lily pads to catch glimpses of the fish.

Looking at the children, Ruthie thought angrily, that should have been us. We should have come here; we should have gone ice-skating again, signed each other's autograph books, graduated together, and been at pajama parties discussing boys.

It's gone. The years we lost are lost forever.

Ruthie looked at Mitzi, thinking of all she'd been through—stared at through a fence, everything taken from her, trying to get an education without real teachers or books. . . .

"How . . . did you . . . I mean, what made you . . . start talking again?" Ruthie asked.

Mitzi walked a few steps closer to the white lilies in the pond.

"I don't know exactly," she said, "but I noticed Uncle Joe wasn't like my dad. Uncle Joe was hurt, too, but he would talk about the people here who helped him, people who were holding his things and were writing—people like you, Ruthie, who couldn't understand how something like this could happen. He wasn't bitter.

"One day, I guess, I asked him why.

" 'Mitzi,' he said, 'when you hate you become like the people who've hurt you.'

"I thought about that," Mitzi said. "And then when Sab got discharged and visited us, he said, 'Mitzi, you have to help Mommy now that Daddy's so down. And you have to help Daddy to stop hating, too.' "

Mitzi blinked and looked at Ruthie.

"Oh, Mitzi," Ruthie cried, unable to hold back, throwing her arms around her. "I'm so sorry. OH, MITZI! I MISSED YOU!"

"ME, TOO, RUTHIE, ME, TOO!" Mitzi said, hugging her back.

They hugged and hugged.

Behind them parents called to children and children called to parents and people told others to smile for the camera.

Finally the girls pulled back and wiped their eyes.

"Mitzi," Ruthie said. "It's over now."

Mitzi looked hard at Ruthie. "The sign outside," she said, "still says 'Chinese Tea Garden.' "

Ruthie rolled her eyes. "Oh, I know," she said, "but Mitzi, things will change."

224

Mitzi said nothing but looked at Ruthie with her dark, dark eyes.

Above them rose the Moon Bridge, curved against the sky, as pennies dropped from the hands of children making wishes.

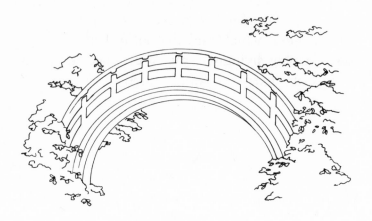

Afterword

When the Japanese government, regarded at the time as a friendly nation, launched a surprise attack on December 7, 1941, at the naval base in Pearl Harbor in the Hawaiian Islands, they wiped out the Pacific Fleet and nearly the entire United States Navy. Feelings of shock and betrayal ran high. The strong prejudice already existing against Asians—especially on the West Coast—became fierce against Japanese-Americans.

Japanese living in America were considered to be loyal to Japan in spite of the fact that many

226

had been residents for generations. In the spring of 1942, President Roosevelt signed Executive Order 9066, which said that all people of Japanese ancestry living on the West Coast "will be evacuated from their homes" in the coming months.

The decree covered those living in Washington, Oregon, and California, but not Hawaii—a territory much closer to Japan. (Hawaii was not yet a state.) The government argued that this step was necessary to protect our defense plants in the coastal states. They feared that Japanese-Americans would discover our military secrets and radio them to Tokyo.

Asians in America have experienced a long history of discrimination. The Chinese Exclusion Law of 1882, which included Japanese, stated that "Orientals" could not become citizens. (All children born in the United States automatically are citizens.) So when one-hundred-and-twenty thousand people—many of them citizens—were locked up in Assembly Centers, few Americans objected.

The evacuees were given less than a week in which to dispose of everything they owned except what would fit in a suitcase. Farms, stores, houses were sold or given away, along with cars, refrigerators, furniture, and pets. The richest farmland in the world in the San Joaquin and Sacramento valleys, which Japanese settlers had worked from arid land, was sacrificed to eager banks.

On the appointed day, the *Issei* (Ih-say) (Japanese born), *Nisei* (Nih-say) (first-generation American born), and *Sensei* (Sahn-say) (second-generation American born) stood in front of their former homes, waiting for army trucks. They were taken to ten Assembly Centers quickly set up outside the big coastal cities, some on former fairgrounds and two—Tanforan and Santa Anita—in former race tracks.

Because the decision to evacuate "aliens"—as the Japanese-Americans were called—had been made hastily without adequate planning, the centers often lacked proper plumbing, food, supplies for babies, and medical supplies for the sick and elderly. Entire families lived in tiny partitions with minimal furniture. Bathing and dining were communal. Barbed wire surrounded the centers; soldiers with rifles stood on guard. Anyone trying to escape was shot.

Within a few months, permanent camps were ready in the neighboring mountain states of Nevada, Wyoming, Colorado, and Idaho on semi-arid land. Two more camps were set up in

Arkansas—on muddy land. All were far from civilization.

There the internees stayed for three years until the war was nearly over in January 1945.

In the years that followed, most internees never spoke of their experiences, not even to their children born after internment. Japanese culture teaches its people to accept shame in silence. The internees had done nothing wrong but many felt shamed by being singled out and locked away. Also, they had already been accused of disloyalty. To criticize the government might seem to prove it.

For these reasons and because the government never discussed what happened, for many years the camps were forgotten. Then in the 1970s, when many groups demonstrated against racial intolerance, the Japanese-Americans spoke out. Committees for Redress were formed. Hearings were held before Congress to let people testify about what they had endured. Many Americans learned for the first time how their country had treated its own people during the war.

The internees and their children asked for financial redress for their losses and for an apology from their government.

On August 10, 1988, forty-three years after the camps were closed, Congress passed Public Law 100-383, which stated:

The purposes of this Act are to:
1) acknowledge the fundamental injustice of the evacuation, relocation, and internment of United States citizens and permanent resident aliens of Japanese ancestry during World War II;
2) apologize on behalf of the people of the United States for the evacuation, relocation, and internment of such citizens and permanent resident aliens;
3) provide for a public education fund to finance efforts to inform the public about the internment of such individuals so as to prevent the recurrence of any similar event;
4) make restitution to those individuals of Japanese ancestry who were interned.

It goes on to say:

With regard to individuals of Japanese ancestry, the Congress recognizes that . . . a grave injustice was done to both citizens and permanent resident aliens of Japanese ancestry. . . . As the Commission documents, these actions were carried out without adequate security reasons and without any acts of espionage or sabotage documented by the Commission, and were motivated largely by racial prejudice, wartime hysteria, and a failure of political leader-

ship. The excluded individuals of Japanese ancestry suffered enormous damages, both material and intangible, and there were incalculable losses in education and job training, all of which resulted in significant human suffering for which appropriate compensation has not been made. For these fundamental violations of the basic civil liberties and constitutional rights of these individuals of Japanese ancestry, the Congress apologizes on behalf of the nation.

Funds were set aside to reimburse the internees still living. At the time of this writing, most still have not been paid since Congress has not appropriated the money.

About the Author

Marcia Savin is a native of San Francisco. She attended UC Berkeley (BA) and San Francisco State (MA).

Ms. Savin writes, "The idea for THE MOON BRIDGE arose from an incident in my life. During World War II in San Francisco, I came upon a group of younger children in the school yard taunting a new girl. They were calling her 'Jap' and yelling 'Go back to Japan.' I ran up and yelled at them to stop, that she was an American like they were. . . . I never forgot the terror in the little girl's eyes.

"This memory, combined with a lifelong love of the Japanese Tea Garden, sparked the idea for THE MOON BRIDGE."

The author lives in Brooklyn with her husband. She has two grown children, and likes opera, old movies, mysteries, and the blues.